Evie

Annie Seaton

Pentecost Island 5

ANNIE SEATON

DEDICATION

To the wonderful girlfriends

I have made through my writing... author and

readers alike!

Chapter One

Evie

Evie Asquith rocked back on her heels and surveyed the new seedlings she'd planted in the warm earth at the resort end of Red Wave Wall track. One thing about being up in the tropics, the plants would double in size within a week, and flower in a month. She'd pulled out all the stops and was working longer days since Pippa and Rafe had announced their wedding date. Six weeks would give her just enough time to get the colour going around the lawn adjacent to the bar where the ceremony would be held.

With a sigh, Evie pushed herself to her feet, her leg muscles pulling. At first light today, she'd climbed the mountain as far as Red Wave Wall. For some reason she'd been unsettled, and the walk to the top of the hill, and the magnificent view over the Passage as the sun had coloured the sky in soft pink and apricot hues, had calmed her. Followed by a solid morning of planting and digging, her equilibrium had been restored.

She knew what was wrong with her. The air was thick with romance, and she was wondering if it was time to move on. Evie didn't need to be reminded of the past; seeing her friends at the resort so happy was tugging at her memories and reminding her of her time with Jed.

Then the guilt had kicked in and she'd had a sleepless night, thus the walk up the mountain at sunrise.

She gathered up her small spade and the now-empty fertiliser bags and headed back to the house for some lunch. A chat with Sienna—the only other single person on the island—would do the trick; maybe they could go over to Hamilton Island for another night soon. As Evie headed towards the huts, her breath caught. A tall man with dark hair was walking along the beach at the water's edge, his head down as he walked towards the rocks. It could have been Jed.

With a sigh, Evie shook her head, and focused on the gardens along the edge of the path. Many times, since she'd left him, she'd thought she'd seen Jed Stephenson. But he was hundreds of kilometres away from this island where she had finally found peace.

Every two years he would pop up somewhere and touch base with her, trying to talk her into accessing the money he'd given her, and, on two occasions, to try to reconcile.

Not that reconciliation was the right word. They weren't estranged; their interactions when he did track her down were amicable, but always brief. Evie just couldn't be with him.

Jed was immersed in his mining career in the Hunter Valley, and the last she'd heard from her friend, Belinda—the only person from her old life she'd kept in touch with—he'd worked his way to the top. He never spoke of himself or work when he caught up with her; it was always about Evie and whether she was okay financially, and happy.

She forced herself to look away from the man on the beach. She didn't need to conjure Jed into her tropical paradise. It sure wasn't wishful thinking; Jed was the last person she wanted to see. She thought she'd been unsettled this morning; seeing Jed would send her into the past, and that would take days to get over.

She sighed and kept walking, smiling as Tam's giggle, followed by Gabe's deep laugh, reached her when she passed the hut they were staying in. It was good to hear Tam laughing. Gabe seemed like a decent enough guy; he was making Tam happy and that was all that mattered.

She paused at the garden of the first hut and

reached down to pull a weed that had already tangled itself around the latticework screen beside the door. As Evie stood and stepped back onto the path, she noticed the guy was coming up from the beach and heading towards the huts.

With a quick sidestep, she detoured onto the narrow path that led through the small forest to the house.

How nice would it have been if her life with Jed had worked out? They would have been married ten years now, and probably would have had a couple of kids.

Don't go there.

With a firm shake of her head, Evie muttered her mantra to herself. 'Life is good.'

Here she was on a tropical island, doing what she loved, and with her own boat to travel the Pacific whenever the whim took her. She was saving well with this current job and she'd caught up with some old friends and made new ones on Pentecost Island.

Yes, I'm happy.

'Eva! Wait!'

The man's voice was deep, and the intonation all too familiar. The way he called her real name was confirmed her suspicions.

Evie tensed.

Well, she had been happy a few seconds ago.

'Stop there . . . please.'

She stood motionless, wishing she could just keep on walking, but she knew she had to respond.

He never gave up.

Evie let go of the spade, and it and the weeds fell unnoticed to the ground as she looked up into the deep blue eyes of her ex-husband.

Chapter Two

Tamsin

Tamsin Jones stretched and lifted her face to the sun. The day was perfect—warm, no wind, the sea was sparkling, and she was cuddled up to Gabe in the double hammock outside the hut they'd shared for the past few days. It rocked precariously as she sat up. 'I don't know if I want to go back to the kitchen tomorrow.'

'I don't want to leave Pentecost Island,' Gabe said softly as he put a hand out to steady the rocking of the canvas bed. 'It's cast a spell on me.'

'Ah, so it's the island that's the attraction. And here I thought it was me you were here to see.' Tamsin put on a mock pout as she looked down at him. She hadn't been this relaxed or happy for a long time.

He answered by putting a gentle hand around the back of her neck and pulling her down to him. A pair of warm lips settled on hers and then there wasn't any talking for a while.

Tamsin moved away and ran her fingers up Gabe's arm. 'I'll miss you when you're not on the island. I've kind of got used to having you around.

Although we are going to be really busy with the work that's about to begin.'

The construction at Ma Carmichael's resort on Pentecost Island was about to ramp up, with planning for more huts, a restaurant, and a day spa well underway.

'It sure is moving fast. The organisation of this place is impressive,' Gabe said. 'I know you'll be busy with the restaurant so I'll try and get over most weekends, that's if I can find a bed to share.' His grin was cheeky, and the butterflies in Tamsin's tummy fluttered in response.

'My room's not as luxurious as this hut,' she said.

'I don't know about that, it has a beautiful woman in it.'

'Flattery will get you everywhere, Gabe Brown.'

'Seriously, Tamsin Jones. I will miss you. It's going to be hard for you to get away for a while.'

'I love how you call me that.' Tam smiled. 'Once we get up and running there'll be a couple more chefs on board, so I'll have more time off. I'm actually thinking of hiring them before Pippa and Rafe's wedding so we can get the teamwork going.'

'Good idea.'

'The only thing holding me back is the thought of professionals trying to work in the current kitchen. But I'll sort it, and I will get over to Hamo more often than you think.'

'Excellent. Nat said he's got a lot of work for me too, so the weekdays will go quickly.'

After Gabe and Tamsin had sorted out the differences that had been a part of them getting to know each other, Tam had introduced him to Nat Dwyer, the partner of her friend, Nell, who was office manager at Ma Carmichael's resort. Nat had been looking for someone to help him in his IT business, and Gabe had walked into the job after leaving his job as a private investigator in Melbourne. The two of them had found a three-bedroom apartment on Hamilton Island to rent together.

'I'm so pleased you'll be close by,' Tam said. 'And if we ever need anything from Hamo, I'll get Evie to run me over. We enjoyed our break over there, and it had an excellent outcome.' She dropped a brief kiss on Gabe's lips. 'Fancy a sandwich? An early lunch?'

His grin was wicked. 'And then maybe an afternoon nap?'

'I'll go and make us—' Tam's words were cut

off by a shrill scream further along the path to the house.

The hammock rocked as Gabe rolled out, and Tamsin grabbed the sides and sat up.

'Who the hell was that?' she said as she jumped out.

'No, no, no.' The scream was followed by shrill words.

'It's Evie, quick, she needs help.'

'No!' Evie was about fifty metres way from them, screaming at the man standing in front of her. 'I won't.'

'What's going on there?' Gabe grabbed his T-shirt and pulled it over his head.

'I don't know who he is.'

'It's the guy staying in the first hut. He arrived on this morning's boat.' Gabe hurried after Tamsin as she ran to the path. 'He checked in when you were over looking at the plans with Pippa and Eliza.'

'Quick.' Tam frowned as they approached Evie and the guy. 'There's something very wrong.'

Evie was crouched on the ground, rocking on her heels as sobs shuddered through her. The stranger was standing over her, his hands spread wide almost in supplication. 'Please, Eva, you have to.'

Gabe stepped in and took the guy's arm, pulling him away as Tamsin crouched on the ground beside Evie.

'Sweetie, it's okay, Gabe and I are here to protect you. What's wrong? What did he do?'

'Tam, can you come with me to my b—take me home? Please.' Evie's voice broke and Tam glanced down as her friend's fingers pressed into her forearm. As she reached out to help Evie up, Tam caught her breath, shocked by the sudden change in her appearance. Her lips were bloodless, and all the colour had leached from her tanned face. Tears filled her eyes, and her voice was almost childlike as she gripped Tamsin's arm. Evie's teeth were chattering as though it was a cold winter's day, not a brilliant spring day on a tropical island.

As Tamsin helped her friend stand, she shot a glance at her partner. 'Gabe, can you sort this while I take Evie away?' Tam frowned at the stranger who had brought Evie to her knees.

Literally.

He was tall and broad shouldered, and even though he'd looked at Evie with concern, he now returned Tamsin's stare with a set expression. His eyes were dark and hooded, but she could sense the emotion rolling off him. It was obvious that he had scared the living daylights out of Evie.

Evie had worked on the island with the girls for a few months now, and Tam had not once seen her lose her cool. Not that her present state could be dismissed so lightly; this was way more than losing her cool. If Tamsin didn't know better, she would say that Evie was in shock.

Gabe nodded. 'You go with Evie, Tamsin. I'll sort this.' He turned to the dark-haired guy beside him.

Tamsin stared at the stranger and was surprised when his voice cracked.

'Eva, please. Stay. You have to listen to me.' He was a similar age to Gabe, Tamsin thought, and to his credit, concern returned to his expression as she turned away to help Evie up.

Evie's husky voice was low and controlled as she clung to Tam. 'Go away, Jed. And my name's Evie.'

Tamsin and Gabe exchanged a glance.

Okay, so Evie knew the guy; he wasn't some random stranger who had hassled her. As Tamsin looked at him, Evie pulled away from her hold and took off into the bush.

'I'll go after her.' Tamsin ran back to the sun

lounge, slipped on her thongs, picked up a beach towel and her sarong, and took off up the bush track after Evie. She must be heading for the back of the island where her boat was anchored.

Tam and Nell lived in the old house that had been on the island when Pippa had inherited it earlier in the year. Sienna, Eliza's friend was staying there with them at the moment, and it looked like she'd soon be joining them to work on the island too.

Pippa had moved out recently and was living with her fiancé in the house on top of the hill across the bay. Eliza, their resident carpenter, lived on a boat in the front bay with her partner, Phillipe. Evie sometimes stayed in the house with the girls, but she preferred to sleep on her boat most nights.

Tamsin picked up her pace. She could hear Evie crashing through the bush ahead of her. Evie had the advantage of sturdy work boots, and Tam's progress in her thongs slowed as the bush thickened and the path petered out.

'Evie, wait up. I'm coming.'

There was no reply.

Tamsin looked around trying to find the path that she'd been on a moment ago. Evie had obviously diverted from the landscaped paths and taken a shortcut through the rainforest. Over the past few months, she'd created a network of paths and small gardens and restful glades in the forest as part of her landscape gardener job at the Ma Carmichael's resort.

'Evie,' Tamsin yelled after her. 'Wait for me.'

Ahead the occasional crack of a branch was getting fainter and Tam tried to go faster. Eventually as she found her way back to the path that led over the hill to Back Bay—where Evie's boat was anchored—the silence was broken only by the soughing of the wind in the top of the hoop pines above her on the hill.

Tam paused, unsure whether to keep going or turn back. Evie was well ahead of her, and this path took a circuitous route to the bay. With a determined sigh, she tied her sarong over her bikini, tucked the towel beneath her arm and kept going; she was too worried about the state Evie had been in to leave her. The path only led to the beach, so she'd come back this way eventually. Hopefully Gabe would go and tell Pippa what had happened once he'd dealt with that guy.

Looking up to the green lacy canopy above, Tamsin could only see a glimpse of the blue sky that she knew was cloudless today. In the glade where she finally re-joined the path, the light was dim. Dropping her gaze, she picked her way along the path, now surrounded by lush vegetation where the lee of the mountain received more rain than the rest of the island. In the mossy crevices of fallen hoop pines, small ferns and creepers poked their green leaves out and the occasional creature scuttled away as she forged ahead.

Eventually Tamsin reached the top of the ridge, where the canopy above was not as thick. She put her hand to her eyes and looked across the bay to where Evie's boat rocked gently on the anchor. There was little wind and the sea was flat, protected from the currents in the Whitsunday Passage on the western side of the island where the resort was located. The sun reflected on the boat's name on the stern.

Kestrel?

When had Evie changed the name of her boat? Tamsin wondered. The first day that Evie had sailed into their bay Pippa had been dismayed by the pink mainsail on Evie's yacht.

Her yacht, *Eros*.

It was definitely Evie's boat; Tamsin had recently been on it, sailing across to Hamilton Island for a few days' break with Evie and Sienna. She hadn't taken much notice of the name on that trip because she'd been stressed on the way over, and then preoccupied with Gabe when they'd returned.

Now, standing on the hill looking down at the boat, Tamsin could see the new name, *Kestrel,* as clear as the blue sky above.

Wasn't it bad luck to change the name of a boat? And why would Evie have changed it?

As Tamsin stood there, trying to decide which of the two paths to take to the beach, a flash of movement on the beach below caught her attention.

A dark-haired figure ran out of the bush, across the sand and onto the rocks. As Tam stood there and watched, Evie pulled off her shirt and work boots and flung them onto the rocks that edged the bay. Then to Tamsin's shock, Evie jumped off the rocks and into the bay.

Tamsin stood there with her hand pressed to her mouth in horror. The water churned as Evie struck out towards the yacht sitting two hundred metres out in the bay. The tender that Evie always took to get to her boat was at the jetty around near the resort.

What the hell had happened back at the huts for Evie to take this huge risk? She could have gone to the jetty and taken the small rubber tender around.

The bay she was swimming across was notorious for sharks, and the stinger season had begun a couple of months ago. Box jelly fish and Irukandji were always a risk in these tropical waters. Pippa had put signs on all the beaches around the island stating that swimming was not permitted without stinger suits.

Not that a suit would protect you from a hungry shark, Tam thought as Evie reached the halfway point and stopped swimming.

Her heart jumped into her throat and she took a deep breath, trying to stay calm as Evie trod water in the middle of the bay. Never in her life had Tamsin felt so utterly helpless. If only she'd thought to get her phone before she'd run after Evie, she could have called for help.

Tamsin blinked and put her hand to her eyes to block the glare reflecting off the water. She scanned the water trying to find the spot where she'd last seen Evie, but there was no sign of her dark head. The water was silver beneath the midday sun . . . and totally calm and empty. Tam waited a minute more, and when there was no sign of her friend swimming, she let out a harsh cry and turned to run back to the resort.

EVIE

Chapter Three
Pippa

Rafe was on the phone to his publisher in the UK, and I was sitting on the balcony surrounded by brochures; brochures for stoves, refrigerators, kitchen appliances and sinks.

When Gabe went back to Hamo tomorrow, the first thing I was going to do was get Tamsin up here to help me order the right appliances for the commercial kitchen. There was always a lag in the delivery time to our island, so we had to get the orders in as soon as we could. Tam had been off with the pixies—the "love" pixies— this morning when she had joined Eliza and I to meet with the Riccardo brothers, our builders. I'd deliberately left her in peace for the first three days of her break with Gabe. I'd never seen her so happy, and I wanted her to have a rest before we got busy.

'Go back and join your man,' I'd said to her with a laugh as I caught her staring down at the huts. 'We can do this without you.'

Tam had shaken her head. 'No, this is my

restaurant. I want to see how big it's going to be when it's pegged out. It's exciting.' Her cheeks were pink, and her stance was relaxed. She'd lost that edginess that had built up over the past few weeks when we'd all been working hard leading up to the bar opening.

It hadn't taken Danny and Renzo Riccardo long to roughly peg out the site.

Tamsin had nodded as she paced it out, and then smiled as she headed back to the beach hut she and Gabe were staying in. 'See you after. Thanks for the time off, Pip. I appreciate it.'

'I can see that,' I'd said with a grin. Eliza and I stayed chatting on the restaurant site when the Riccardos left, until Phillipe came back in the tender to pick her up.

'Love is in the air,' I sang, and Eliza chuckled.

'It's good to see Tam so happy,' she said.

I shook my head as I walked up the hill. The speed at which the building was going ahead was very pleasing. The buildings were all open plan, and basic sizes, so construction wasn't complicated, Danny had assured me when he'd looked at our plans.

Hopefully the building should be finished in time for the wedding.

My wedding. Our wedding.

I couldn't believe Rafe and I were getting married. Sometimes I had to pinch myself to make sure the whole resort thing and Rafe wasn't a dream, and that I wasn't back at the Gold Coast still working in advertising.

But it was no dream, and thanks to my Great-Aunt Vi Carmichael, I was here on Pentecost Island, and had started Ma Carmichael's Resort with my two friends, Tam and Nell. Our first guests had arrived, and the resort was expanding quickly.

On the way back up to the house, I smiled as I thought about our six months on the island. Life had been a whirlwind since Tam, Nell and I had arrived in late autumn.

I'd met Rafe, fallen head over heels after a difficult start to our relationship, and now we were preparing for our wedding. Eliza had arrived, and then Phillipe had turned up, and they'd gone back to Italy for a brief visit to sort out her deceased husband's estate. When Eliza had come back and gone into partnership with me—and then Tam and Nell—the increased capital had meant we could expand immediately.

Nell had reunited with Nat, and they were as happy as two lovebirds. And now Tam's trip to

Hamilton Island before our bar opening last week had resulted in her meeting Gabe—albeit under strange circumstances—but it had certainly made me reconsider the term "love at first sight".

As I waited for Rafe to finish his call, I sighed and put my head back.

Closing my eyes, I listened to the pretty calls of the tropical birds in the trees along the pool fence. Being constantly happy was a totally new way of life for me, and I must admit to wondering if it could last sometimes. Life here on the island was wonderful and I would never forget Aunty Vi or forget how grateful I was to her for leaving half of Pentecost Island to me in her will.

Life was about to get a lot busier, and I made a mental list as the sun warmed my face.

One. Talk to Tam about the appliances.

Two. See Nell about whether we should keep the three huts open while the others were being built. I shook my head. That was a yes. Of course, we would.

Three. Chase up the name signs for the huts. Huts One, Two and Three, didn't sound very exotic.

Four. Talk to Sienna about the size of the treatment rooms in the day spa. And sort out whatever visas she needed to be able to stay on the island. And think of a name for the day spa and order the sign.

Five. Remember to talk to Tam about a menu for our wedding. A squiggle of excitement tickled at the thought of marrying my gorgeous Rafe. We were going to stay on the island until the construction was finished and we were up and running with full capacity, and then we were going to go on our honeymoon next autumn. Rafe was going to take me to his home in the UK spring.

The wedding was the current priority; Everything else would fall into place. I had confidence in my team. Having Tam and Nell, Eliza, Evie and Sienna—Eliza's friend and our future day spa therapist—here had made the planning, and consequently my life, so much easier. Even before Nell and Tam had come on board as shareholders—thanks to Eliza's generosity—they had been totally committed to Ma Carmichael's, and I knew Evie was too.

Okay, back to my list.

Six. Offer Cherry and Mirabella permanent shifts.

Seven, and highest priority. Talk to Evie. After two weeks of having guests in the huts, I knew that putting in a pool was one of the first things we had to do. The fear of sharks since the recent attacks at Cid

Harbour, and the reluctance of many tourists to wear the head-to-foot stinger suits—we had a supply in the office—had led to my realisation that we must put a small pool in, at the back of the huts as soon as we could get the pool company over here. Each of the guests who had stayed in the three huts over the past ten days since our opening had put that on their feedback form.

Fabulous resort. Would be perfect with a pool.

Logistically it was going to be a nightmare, but hey, I had no doubt we could do it. Since Eliza had become a business partner, the finances had opened up, and we were going to get the resort completed within a year of opening.

The gate creaked; I opened my eyes and sat up. Rafe had put a small lap pool in at the side of his house for exercise and I looked across it as he walked along the paved edge.

'Want some lunch, love?' he asked.

'Rafe, how hard was it to get your pool over here?' I smiled as he leaned down and kissed me.

He shrugged. 'I don't know. I was in the UK when it was installed. It couldn't have been too hard because I didn't get any calls.'

'But I bet you got a big bill,' I said.

Even though he smiled back at me, he had the grace to colour, and I grinned back at him.

God, I loved this man.

'Um. I didn't have a close look at the breakdown. I just paid the invoice.'

I shook my head and pulled a face at him. 'We—I mean, Ma Carmichael's—look at *all* the bills and *all* the breakdowns. We're not rich like you are.' I leaned back and reached my arms around his neck knowing my teasing would get a response. I loved teasing Rafe; it usually ended up with him tickling me and then moving into the bedroom. I would never take our relationship for granted. I loved this man with my heart and soul.

'So, ham and cheese grill—' he broke off and walked towards the edge of the balcony. 'We've got company, Phillipa.'

I stood and stretched and walked over to stand beside Rafe at the gate. He put his arm around my shoulder, and I leaned into him. My breath caught and held. As soon as I saw Tam and Gabe, I knew something was wrong.

Very wrong.

Chapter Four

Tamsin

When Tam told Pippa how Evie had disappeared when she'd been swimming out to her boat, Pippa shook her head.

'No, she must have stopped to catch her breath, and you just couldn't see her. Why was she swimming out there anyway?'

'The guy in the hut next to us said something to her and she was really upset. I've never seen her like that. Like almost hysterical.'

'What guy?' Pippa frowned as she looked at Tamsin. 'Who? What's his name?'

'I think she called him Jed. But hurry, we need to get around there and . . . and look for her.'

Pippa grabbed Rafe's arm. 'Come on, we'll get your boat and go around to the bay. I'm sure she'll be fine.' Pippa spoke quietly under her breath, but Tamsin heard her words. 'She has to be.'

Gabe took Tamsin's hand and she held it tightly as they all hurried down to the jetty. Her heart was still pounding, and she couldn't get the image of Evie disappearing beneath the water out of her head. Tamsin hitched a sob and Gabe put his arm around her as they reached the sand.

'Just hope for the best, love.' He looked down at Tamsin before turning to Pippa. 'Jed Stephenson, he said his name was, but he wouldn't tell me anymore. Only that he knew Evie and he had a personal matter he had to speak to her about. And he was just as upset as Evie was when she took off. I tried my best to talk to him, but he went back into the hut and shut the door in my face.' Gabe shrugged. 'Apart from beating the door down, there wasn't a lot I could do. So, I took off after Tam and Evie, but I met Tam on the way back.'

They reached the jetty and it was only minutes before Rafe's speedboat was roaring around to the back of the island.

Once they were underway, Tam put her hand on her chest as her throat closed. She swallowed.

'Pip, I didn't know what to do. I felt so bloody useless when I chased her into the forest. She was so upset, I really think she was in shock, and then I saw her take her gear off and try to swim to the boat. What the hell could have upset her so much?'

'I have a bit of an idea what's wrong.' Pippa

stared out over the water. 'It was a long time ago, but I helped Evie out when we were at uni and she told me her story. But she swore me to secrecy.'

'You helped a few of us out back then,' Tam said.

'That's one of the reasons I was so happy to take Evie on here. She's made a whole new life for herself. She's been a lost soul for a long time. A loner.'

'She seemed really happy here. Oh, God, I so hope she's on the boat and everything is okay.'

As they entered the Passage, Rafe increased the speed of the boat, and a white stream of wash fanned out behind the boat.

'When I ran back through the rainforest, I was thinking about her. I've been preoccupied, but I was thinking back. Evie's told me some stuff that hasn't made sense. I remember she told me when she first came that her grandfather gave her the boat, and she'd lived on it eight years, and then I'm sure she said when we went to Hamo a couple of weeks ago she bought it while she was working on Hamo. I didn't take much notice until I was trying to make sense of what happened today.'

Pippa stared past Tam as they reached the northern point of Pentecost Island. 'Evie's carried a lot of guilt for the past few years. I think she's been trying to hide, but . . . but I just want her to be okay.' Pippa's voice broke, and Tam reached out and hugged her.

'Me too.'

They both stared ahead as they reached Back Bay.

Pippa's face broke into a smile as they stared across the empty bay.

'Thank God, for that,' Tam said. 'I think.'

'She's alright,' Pippa said.

Tam nodded. 'Yes, on *Eros* or *Kestrel.* Whatever her boat is called, it's gone.' She was beginning to realise she hadn't known Evie at all.

Rafe took his boat on a circuit around the bay, and as they turned west to head back to the resort, Pippa lifted her arm and pointed.

'Look!'

On the horizon, if she looked hard enough, she could just make out a pink sail.

'Thank God,' Tam said as Gabe put his arm around her. 'What a day!'

Chapter Five
Eva - ten years earlier

'See you at the woolshed, gals,' Melissa, their last customer, called back as nineteen-year-old hairdresser, Evangelina Asquith locked the door behind her. She and Belinda, the apprentice, had been run off their feet in the salon since seven that morning; it seemed like every single female within a hundred kilometres was going to the B&S ball and wanted their hair done today.

'Your turn now, Eva.' Belinda held the cape out.

'I'm buggered,' Eva said as she flopped in the chair and leaned back.

'Sit up,' Belinda said. 'Me too, but a shower and a strong coffee will turn us around. How are you getting out to the woolshed?' she asked as Evie sat up and Belinda brushed her hair out.

The ball was being held fifteen kilometres out of town at one of the biggest stations in the district.

'I'll go with Zeke, and then if I get sick of it early, I'll bring his ute home.'

'You can't do that. You'll miss half the fun.

Aren't you taking your swag to sleep in?'

Eva shrugged. 'I'm sorry, Bin. I just can't get excited about it. I might have lived here all my life, but I really don't enjoy all this country stuff.'

'Go on, you do. You'll be the belle of the ball with this hair do.'

'Not too fancy please,' Eva said as Belinda looped another strand of hair around the crown of her head.

'Oh, come on, Eva. One more curl and that's it. I've been practising this style for weeks.'

Eva folded her arms beneath the black cape and nodded. Belinda was an excellent apprentice, and Eva had volunteered as a guinea pig for the practice run for the B&S ball tonight.

'Just trust me. It will be perfect.' Belinda lifted the curling tongs. 'Close your eyes or I'll put a mask on you, while I put on a bit more colour.'

'You can't put the colour on now.'

'Oh, yes I can. I've been experimenting. In fact,' she said as she reached under the counter. 'You can see the updo when it's baked.'

'Baked?' Eva said on a squeak. 'What sort of an apprentice are you, Belinda Bentley?'

'One with all the new tricks. Now be quiet and close your eyes while I put the mask on, Eva. And to answer your question, I'm also the best apprentice Bylington has ever seen.'

Eva chuckled as the mask slipped over her eyes. 'You're the only apprentice Bylington has ever seen, Binny.'

'Apart from you. Why don't we buy this salon together when I'm qualified? You already are, and old Gloria's past it. You almost run the salon anyway. The new bank manager fancies me, I'm sure I'd get a business loan.'

'It takes more than being "fancied" to get a business loan. And how old are you anyway? "Fancied", for God's sake? That's a Gloria word. You've been here too long.' Eva could imagine Binny's expression even with the mask over her eyes. 'Sorry to rain on your parade, Bin, but the chances of me being in this hick town in another year are zero, zip and non-existent.'

'What! Why?' Belinda's tone held shock.

'Because Reg is okay now; he won't need me here. He's got a job at the mine, Zeke and Samantha are getting married, and Zeke's going back to the farm in a couple of months. I'm not going to be needed. I'm going to be as free as a bird.'

'Oh. You never said a word.'

'I didn't want to jinx it. But it's all happening now, and you won't see me for the dust.'

'Well, there's plenty of that in this town.'

Eva settled back and let Binny do her hair and she didn't argue again. Sometimes she wondered why she was such a misfit in Bylington. Despite having lived on the farm since she was born, she wasn't a country girl at heart.

Eva had always loved the sea, and when she was eight-years-old, she'd told her mother she must have been adopted. 'I don't want to live here, Mummy. I want to be near the sea where Grandpa is.'

Her mother's father lived on a boat and was spending his retirement sailing in the tropics. Whenever he was in Sydney, they'd go down to visit him at the harbour. Well, Mum and Eva did anyway; her big brother, Zeke, wouldn't leave the farm.

'Sorry, sweetheart, you're a country girl, and you're certainly not adopted. I remember very well bringing you home from the hospital,' her mother had replied as she'd deftly braided her hair for school. 'I want you to come straight home from school today as

I'll need help with the baking. The shearers arrive next week, and we have to have enough cake and biscuits for ten days of smokos.'

Eva's throat clogged with unshed tears that still hit her at the strangest times. It was five years since Mum had passed, and she still missed her every day. Being a fourteen-year-old without a mum had been bloody hard.

Being a fourteen year-old with a stepdad who resented her was almost as hard.

Back on that afternoon after the baking was finished, Eva had gone out into the backyard, her school shoes crunching on the dead brown grass under the Hills Hoist. With a glance over her shoulder, she'd shinnied up the metal pole and put her hand to her eyes. Surely if she was up this high, she could see the sea from here.

But all she could see was dry rolling paddocks, with no sign of a harbour, her grandpa, or his boat.

But then Mum had got sick and died, and now Eva was stuck here cooking and cleaning for her stepfather and her older brother when she wasn't at the salon, doing a job that she'd never wanted.

After Mum passed away, she often thought of that afternoon when she climbed the clothesline, and

Eva's yen to be near the sea hadn't lessened.

It seemed that everything in her life was always done to suit someone else. Now that she had qualified as a hairdresser, she would be out of here as soon as she could pick up a job. Dubbo was the closest city to their small town, but she'd had no luck finding a position there so far.

She rolled her eyes and wondered what she was doing. Even looking for a job in Dubbo had been at Zeke and Reg's suggestion.

If you work in Dubbo, you can come home and help out on the weekends.

If I moved far, far away, I wouldn't have to do anything, Eva thought. And then the usual pang of guilt that she was being selfish would always hit.

Eva didn't want to stay on the farm. She wanted to be on the coast. Some of her happiest memories had been in the holidays with Mum and Grandpa on his boat.

When he was in from the sea that was, and then he would tell her stories of pirates, and tropical islands and buried treasure.

'I love living on the edge, chicken,' he would say to her.

'Taking risks, you mean, Grandpa?' she would

ask.

'No.' He'd tap his pipe on the table in the galley, much to Mum's dismay. 'I like to live on the edge of the land and always be near my boat. Living in the middle of the country makes me feel claustrophobic.'

Mum's sister, Aunty Gloria, had offered Eva an apprenticeship after school, and even though she'd qualified for a rural scholarship to go to university in Brisbane, her stepfather had said no.

'Sorry, Evangelina, the farm can't afford it.'

'But I've got a scholarship, Reg.' Calling him Dad had stopped as soon as Mum had gone. Eva had only called him Dad to make her mother happy.

He *wasn't* their father.

'Sorry, we need you here to look after Zeke and me, and what Gloria pays you will come in handy too.'

It was always about the money.

So here she was, almost twenty, still stuck in Bylington, but her escape plan was brewing.

Claustrophobic. Grandpa had nailed it.

Now, Eva put her head back when Belinda pressed her hand on her forehead.

'You've made that solution too strong. I can smell it,' she said.

'Don't be a difficult customer. I'm going to get it just right for you. I've heard that there's a lot of guys from the new mine coming to the ball tonight. I am so excited.'

'Is your bank manager going?" Eva asked with a smile.

##

Eva yawned as she unlocked the front door of the farmhouse she'd always lived in. Zeke was going to the ball and he'd eat there. Reg was on afternoon shift, so she didn't have to cook dinner for anyone. The night was crisp and clear with a zillion stars dotting the sky. In the night when the yellowed paddocks were softened by moonlight, and the heat of the day had gone, Eva could almost cope with being here in the bush.

Standing at the back door looking out into the night, as always she managed to lock her dreams away. Her mood had gone downhill when Belinda had assumed she would stay in Bylington.

Eva reached up and pulled the pins out of her hair. 'Stuff the B & S ball,' she muttered. No matter how nice a night it was, she'd spend the night watching a movie. Flopping on the lounge she kicked off her Doc Martens and picked up the remote. She had a rental

DVD she wanted to watch.

As the television clicked on, Eva knew she wouldn't be going out tonight. Once Belinda had a few drinks, she wouldn't even miss her in the huge crowd at the woolshed and the paddocks.

The rattle of a diesel ute interrupted her television viewing half an hour later, and she pushed herself to her feet and walked into the kitchen to put the jug on. Zeke—her older brother—was a creature of habit and would look for a cuppa as soon as he was through the front door.

'Where are you, Eva? I get first dibs at the bathroom.'

'I'm in the kitchen, and you can have it as long as you want. I've changed my mind, Zeke,' she called out to her brother as he clomped along the wooden veranda. 'I'm not going to the ball.'

'You're bloody coming, Eva.'

'I don't want to go,' she argued. 'I'm tired.'

'What from? Flapping your jaw in an air-conditioned hairdressing salon all day. Jeez, what do you think I've been doing . . . having a picnic in the paddock?'

'I'll think about it.'

'You're coming. Come on, Eva, you'll have a great time. You know you will.' Zeke pulled out two cups and two teabags. 'You can even have the bathroom first.'

'Oh, jeez, thanks.' Eva rolled her eyes.

When they had finished their tea, Zeke stood over her. 'Go and get your glad rags on, sis. It's going to be the best ball yet. I'm meeting Samantha there, so you can still come in my ute.'

'No, Zeke, I'm too tired. We were flat out all day. We had all the girls in plus the usual Saturday appointments. Do you know how awful it is to listen to everything that's happened in this hick town for the last week?'

Their argument was short, but intense, and of course, Zeke ended up getting his own way. He always did.

'You're the one who took over Aunty Gloria's salon, so don't whine about it. Now turn that friggin' TV off and go and get glammed up. It's Saturday night. And it's going to be the biggest and best B&S ball ever, from all accounts.' Zeke winked at her. 'Lots of new guys in town.'

'Anything to keep the peace,' she muttered

beneath her breath. 'Just because you're the eldest don't think you're the boss of me.'

Zeke had grinned at her; he was always happy when he got his own way. Not so happy when he didn't. That was partly the reason why she'd given in; she would have worn his bad mood for a week or more if she hadn't.

'Not up for discussion, sis. It goes without saying. I'm the oldest and I'm the boss.'

She picked up the cushion and pegged it at her brother. 'Okay, I'm only coming because that series was crap. Not because you told me to.'

Zeke's laughter followed her all the way to the bathroom. 'Sure.'

Two hours later, Eva was grateful Zeke had made her go to the ball.

Chapter Six

Jed

Jed Stephenson fell in love with Evangelina Asquith the night he met her; the problem would be convincing her he was serious.

'Jed?' Zeke Asquith, who was his leading hand at the mine had called out to him when he arrived at the B& S ball. 'Come and meet my sister, Evangelina.'

Jed had had a beer with Zeke one afternoon last week, and he'd asked if he was coming to the B&S ball the following Saturday.

'Not my scene, thanks anyway, mate.' Jed had laughed. 'I'm not after a wife.'

'It's not about finding a wife these days.' Zeke chuckled. 'Sam and I are going, and we're already engaged.'

Jed shook his head. 'I haven't got any formal gear with me.'

'Don't need it. That was the old days when it was a formal do. These days anything goes. Fancy dress, jeans and T-shirts, whatever you feel comfortable in. It's a great chance to meet the local community. Some of my mates will come in from properties a hundred kilometres out. There'll be good music, and lots of grog flowing. A hundred bucks a ticket and that includes all you can drink, dinner and breakfast.'

'Ah, the night goes for a long time then,' Jed commented.

'A long time *and* a good time.' Zeke grinned at him.

'Back in my single days I used to think B&S stood for beer and sex. When I was up at a mine in outback Queensland, I heard it stood for "blokes and sheilas",' Jed said with a grin.

'Nah, not these days. But it's a great way to get to know outback Australia. Anyway, Jed, come along tonight. I'll introduce you to some of my friends.'

He'd been swayed and one look at the gorgeous face, big brown eyes, and rose-red lips of Zeke's sister and Jed was pleased he'd come along. Very pleased. He was a goner.

Evangelina was drop-dead gorgeous and she'd agreed to have the first dance with him, and through fair means and foul—it helped when you were the boss of a lot of the blokes at the ball—she was still dancing with him at midnight when the fireworks started.

'Please call me Eva,' she'd said. 'I hate my full name.' Her voice was as sweet as she was, and Jed had nodded like a lovestruck teenager.

'I think it's a pretty name,' Jed had replied. Every time some other guy tried to cut in, he gave them the evil eye.

Eva's hair was dark, long and straight with a white-blonde streak that fanned across her forehead when she put her head down. She was tall—not far below his six foot—and Jed found it hard to stop looking at her.

Finally, after hours of dancing, with frequent breaks for water, Eva grabbed his hand and dragged him over to sit on the front of a bright blue ute to watch the fireworks.

'Yours?' he asked with a smile.

'No, it's Zeke's, but I'm going to take it and head home soon. I've had a big day. I was tired and now you've worn me out dancing.'

He couldn't help lifting his hand and pushing back that white streak of hair. 'I've had a great time, thank you.' Jed felt Eva jump as a large crack came from behind the ute. He put his arm around her as she laughed. 'What the hell was that?' he said looking around. 'That wasn't fireworks.'

'Just some of the boys having a whip-cracking competition. Things'll get pretty rowdy from now on. The food dye will start flowing soon too.'

'Food dye?'

'Did you see that guy with VIRGIN written on his forehead before?' To his satisfaction Evangelina hadn't moved away when he put his arm around her.

'Yeah, I did,' Jed replied.

'Well, that's red food dye, and it's because it's his first B&S ball. He's a ball virgin.' Her lips tilted in a cheeky smile and his heart thumped. 'Hey, is this your first?'

'Don't even think about it,' he said with a chuckle.

'Well, don't let it be known or you'll be marked too.' Eva covered her mouth with her hand as she yawned. 'And then about three o'clock everyone will crash in their swags—or on the ground—and then at dawn, the barbie will light up and the beer will flow again.' There was a dull note in her voice, and he looked at her curiously.

'You sound like it's something you're not fussed about.'

She nodded. 'You're spot on. I only came because Zeke dragged me along. But I did have fun, thanks. You're a good dancer. Now I'm ready for bed.'

Jed tried to block the thought of Eva in bed, but the couple of beers he'd had earlier let his imagination run wild. He looked away from her and took his arm from around her shoulders. 'Anyway, if you're leaving, I'll head home as well,' he said.

'Where did you park?' she asked. 'A lot of those cars will be parked in for the night by now.' She gestured to the huge paddock behind them. It was full of utes, trucks and four wheel drives.

He shook his head. 'I got a lift out. I heard there were buses running back to town every hour. I'll go back to the pickup point.'

Happiness surged through him at her next words. 'No need to do that. Jump in. I'll run you back to town.' Her slow smile set his nerve endings on fire.

Everywhere.

***

'A bit of local knowledge goes a long way,' Eva said as she glanced at Jed when he climbed into the passenger seat of Zeke's ute. 'Even if it's a long way from the action, you always park at one end of the

48

parking rows. That way you can't get parked in.'

'Smart move.'

She didn't look at him as he spoke. Jed had the most gorgeous deep voice, and she'd been trying to block the instant attraction she'd felt from the moment Zeke had introduced them. It didn't help that he was tall and broad-shouldered and good looking, with the longest eyelashes she'd ever seen on a man. His eyes were a deep blue, set in a tanned face, and further accentuated by his dark hair. He reminded her of one of those guys on that farmer reality TV show.

'The Farmer Wants a Wife,' she murmured to herself.

'Sorry? What was that?' He looked at her curiously.

'Nothing. I was just thinking aloud. So, you work at the mine?' she asked casually as she started the engine. 'How long have you been there?'

'This is my third week. Zeke said it would be a good chance to meet some people tonight.'

'You didn't meet many.' Heat ran into her cheeks as he glanced over at her.

'I enjoyed meeting you,' he said.

'Ditto. Nice to talk to someone who knows a bit

more than Bylington.'

'How long have you been here?' he asked. 'It seems like a decent town.'

'You think?' She pushed the gearstick harder than she needed to. 'It's the most boring place on earth. I was born here, and I can't wait to get out.'

'Oh?'

She was gratified to hear disappointment in Jed's voice.

'You're leaving? When?'

With a sigh, she let off the hand brake. 'As soon as I can get a job.'

'What sort of work do you do?'

'I'm a hairdresser. It's not what I wanted to do. I got roped into it. A family business. I was needed at home, so I had to stay here.'

'What did you want to do?

'I wanted to go to uni in Brisbane.'

'Cities aren't all they're cracked up to be, you know. I grew up in Brisbane and I went to uni there.' Jed's voice was soothing as they turned onto the main road that would take them the fifteen kilometres back to town.

'I'd give anything to get away from here. It's

confining.' She shrugged. 'I guess I sound like a whiner, but you asked.'

'How do you mean?' Jed had turned his head to look at her, and a wave of self-consciousness flooded through her. The moon was full and there was enough light for her to be aware of his intense scrutiny.

'I'll tell you about it one day.' Eva swallowed. There was no way she'd admit it but suddenly being here didn't seem so bad. 'Are you hungry?' She turned her head and shot him a grin, again conscious of that warmth that ran through her whenever Jed looked at her. 'You didn't eat anything there, did you?'

'No, I was kept too busy dancing with a certain lady who kept on saying, "Oh, this is my favourite song." You have a lot of favourites.'

Eva giggled. 'Well, it was great music. Even a city boy would have to admit that it was a great Aussie rock selection.'

'I decline to answer on the grounds it might get me into trouble, and then you won't go out with me when I ask you.'

This time, it was pure heat that ran up her neck and down into her lower belly, and her reply was soft. 'When you ask me?'

She caught the flash of a smile before he nodded. 'Yes, when I ask you. But before I can do that, I'll have to find out where the best restaurant is in town.'

Eva couldn't hold back her giggle. 'That's not hard. You have the choice of the Chinese at the bowling club, the fish and chip takeaway, or the bistro at the one and only pub. The Royal Hotel.'

'Okay,' he said slowly. 'If you had to choose what would you pick?'

'Right now? I'd choose the pie at Jim's caravan on the other side of town.'

'Will it still be open? He glanced at his watch. 'It's after midnight.'

'Jim'll be open all night and he'll do a roaring trade as the early leavers head home. He makes the best mushy peas, and his wife makes the pies. He only opens his van when the B&S is on, and the footie finals.'

'Yum. You've convinced me. If I ask you nicely will you take me there?'

Eva nodded. 'Even if you didn't want to go, I'd be swinging by there on the way home. I'm starving.'

'Okay, consider it our first date. Pies and mushy peas from a caravan.'

Chapter Seven

Jed

As far as first dates went, Jed and Eva's first date was a rip-roaring success. The pies had been amazing—Jed was surprised when Eva lined up for a second pie when he did—and the company was great.

Their second date was the following night at the bowling club, the third the night after that at the pub bistro, and tonight a fish and chip takeaway on a picnic rug on the banks of the Macquarie River.

Eva licked the salt and grease from her fingers as she looked out over the river. For a small shop so far from the coast, it was the best fish and chips Jed had ever tasted.

'Well, Jed, I'm sorry to say we're done now.' She looked at him through the white swathe of fringe that fell over her face as she lay back on the picnic rug.

Disappointment shafted through him. 'Done? What do you mean *done*?'

'You've experienced all the fine dining there is to be had in Bylington. There's nowhere else to go.' She looked up at him from underneath her lashes. 'Unless . .

,

'Unless?' Jed asked moving across the picnic rug, so he was closer to her. Her tone was playful, and he realised she was teasing him.

'Unless you're willing to try my cooking.'

He rolled over onto his stomach and propped his chin on his hand. Her face was only a few centimetres from his and he was pleased when she didn't move away. 'I think that sounds pretty good to me.' He moved a little closer.

'I just have one question,' she asked.

'Hmm?'

Her eyes sparkled as his lips hovered over hers. 'Would it be okay if I cooked for you at your place. You sure don't want to share the dinner table with Zeke and my stepfather at the farm.'

He pretended to frown. 'I think I could put up with you cooking at my place. What would *you* say if I asked you one question?' Her lips were almost touching his and her breath warmed his lips as she answered.

'My answer would be yes.'

He brushed his lips across hers and smiled against her mouth. 'You don't even know the question. I was going to ask if you'd stay the night.'

'My answer would still be yes.'

***

The past four days had been the happiest of Eva's life since Mum had died. For the first time she wasn't at someone's beck and call doing what *they* wanted her to do. The enjoyment she took from Jed's company was right up there with being on Grandpa's boat. Her determination to leave town was fading by the day, and the more time she spent in Jed's company, the less time she spent looking at jobs online.

As Jed's lips pressed against hers, she closed her eyes and gave herself up to his kiss. It was different being with someone who didn't want to boss her around and criticise her every action. When Jed suggested something, he always asked her if it was alright with her. That was a novel experience after living with Reg and Zeke. Even Aunty Gloria tried to tell her what to do when she came into town.

When Jed pulled back and held her gaze with his, a sense of contentment settled in her.

'You make me feel like myself,' she said.

His smile was gentle, but he frowned. 'How do I do that? What do you mean?'

'You let me be me,' she said simply. Eva

reached up and pulled his head back down to hers.

Chapter Eight

Pippa

Tamsin followed me off the jetty looking morose. After we came back from the bay and Tam made us all lunch, Rafe took Nat and Gabe over to Hamilton Island. As well as taking on two big contracts, they were moving into the apartment they were sharing that afternoon. Nell had been busy on the phone and had said her goodbyes to Nat at the house, but she and Nat were used to him coming and going to the island now.

Not Tam. This was their first farewell.

Poor Tam looked like she was about to cry.

'The week will fly, Tam. It'll be the weekend before you know it, and he'll be back. And I'm going to keep you busy, so you won't have time to brood.'

'It's all right for you, Pippa.' She nudged me as she stepped into the sand. 'You've got Rafe here with you all the time.'

'I know. And I love every minute of it.' I tried not to sound too smug.

'Nell said the rest of tonight's guests are coming

back with Rafe.'

'Yeah, saves Jiminy a trip. We're booked up for another month.'

Jed was the only guest on the island until the boat came back.

'Did he order some lunch?' I asked as we walked towards the huts. 'Hut One, I mean. I have to chase those signs up.'

'Gabe knocked on his door before, while I was making the sandwiches, but he didn't answer. He thought the guy might have been out walking.'

'Looking for Evie, I'd say,' I said.

'Do you think she'll come back, Pippa?' Tam asked.

'I sure hope so. It's going to be hard to get someone with a work ethic and skills like Evie's at short notice. Rafe can mow, but the landscaping is beyond him: he doesn't know a spade from a garden fork.' I chuckled. 'And as well as helping me get the wedding organised, he's got to get the proposal for this new book to his publisher in the next couple of weeks.'

Tam bit her lip as she looked at me. 'What's your gut feeling about Evie?'

I stopped walking and stared out over the water.

There was a lot of boating activity out there today, but no sign of a pink sail. 'Evie's a good person, and I don't think she'll just take off. She won't leave us in the lurch. She'll be back.'

'Do you think she'll call and let us know? I could try and message her on Facebook,' Tam offered. 'I didn't really know her that well before we went over to Hamo for our break, but we really hit it off there and I saw a different side to her. She usually keeps to herself, but she opened up and we had fun. Did you know she used to be a hairdresser?'

'I won't breach her confidence, but she'd had some issues before we met her at uni. She made a very hard decision, and it impacted on her in a big way. When she contacted me about working here, I thought she had her act together.' I tapped my lip and frowned. 'She did. I know she did. It was just Jed turning up that's really thrown her.'

'More than thrown her, Pip. It was almost as though someone had died. It's hard to describe the state she was in. Whatever he said to her obviously came as a huge shock. You should have seen her.'

'I've got a feeling she'll be out of range, but I'll try and call her. I'll ask Nell how long Jed's booked in for. I can tell Evie when he's going, and then she can stay away until he's gone.'

'I got the feeling that she didn't want him to know she was on a boat,' Tam said. 'She changed what she was going to say and asked me to take her *home*, not to the boat.'

'I don't even know that Jed knew she's still got her grandfather's boat.'

'Ah, so it was her grandfather's,' Tam said.

'Yes, that's no secret.'

'You don't think so? I wondered if she'd changed the name so anyone who was looking for her couldn't find her.'

'You might be right, you know, and if he doesn't know about her living on her boat, he would have thought she's still on the island.' I frowned, wondering about Evie's over the top reaction. Evie had told me that Jed caught up with her every couple of years and it hadn't seemed as though she'd been upset like she was this time.

Tam nodded thoughtfully. 'He probably does think that.' Gabe said he saw him heading off towards Red Wave Wall after we got back. Maybe he thought there were more houses over there.'

'Maybe.'

'I took him a breakfast tray this morning, and I actually felt sorry for him. He looked really sad. Do you know who he is, Pip? And why he would be here looking for Evie?'

'Can you keep this to yourself? If you're dealing with Jed, you should know, and if Evie comes back, I'll tell her that I told you.' I paused and looked over at the huts but there was no sign of life.

Tam waited for me to speak.

'Jed Stephenson is Evie's ex-husband.'

Chapter Nine

Eva - ten years earlier

As well as being a gentleman, Jed Stephenson was straight and true. What you saw was what you got. There was no gameplaying, and he made it quite clear to Eva the first night she stayed at his house that he was in love and he intended marrying her one day.

'What?' Eva widened her eyes when he said that, between the roast dinner and the apple crumble she'd cooked in his state-of-the-art kitchen. She dropped her fork on the floor, but to her credit, she didn't spit any food when her jaw dropped.

Because Eva knew Jed was sincere, she really didn't know what to say, because he was the best thing that had ever happened to her.

Looking at him now, she snapped her mouth shut. His smile was that usual gentle smile she was quickly getting used to.

Was it only five days since they'd met? It seemed as though she'd known him for much longer. Eva was totally comfortable with Jed; he was so different to any of the local boys she'd gone out with after high school.

'That is only for your information.' He lifted his hand. 'You don't have to say anything. I just wanted you to know what I was thinking. I'm not going to rush you, Eva. We'll let it take as long as it takes.'

'As long as it takes?' Eva shook her head, dazed. 'You don't even know me.'

'Do you think I haven't told myself that every night this week? This is new to me too. I'm trying to get used to how I feel. When I'm with you, I feel right.'

Eva nodded slowly. 'I know exactly what you're saying. It does feel right when we're together. Like I said, I feel like me. And I don't feel like that very often.'

Their gazes met and held, and Eva's appetite fled as her stomach did somersaults.

'So now I've got that out of the way,' Jed asked with that gorgeous smile.

##

Eva spent at least two nights a week sleeping at Jed's house, but he wouldn't let her move in, even though she'd suggested they could give it a try.

He was adamant when she raised it three months into their relationship. Because that's what they had now—a relationship. Eva had accepted that.

'When you move into our house, it will be as my wife. None of this casual living together stuff.' He curled her hair around his finger. The white fringe had grown out, and she'd refused to let Belinda colour her hair again. She'd asked Jed what he liked, and his reply had been simple. 'It's your hair, whatever you choose I'll love.'

She'd reached over and tickled him. 'Okay, red and yellow stripes then.'

'If it makes you happy.'

Eva rolled her eyes. 'You're hopeless. I'm not used to this. I've always had to do what Reg and Zeke wanted.'

'They told you what colour to dye your hair?'

'No, silly. They told me what to do in the big things. Like a job, and where I lived and why I couldn't go to uni. Like I told you, the last thing I wanted was to be a hairdresser.'

Jed rested his forehead against hers. 'I don't want you ever to feel like I'm telling you what to do. It's not a healthy way to have a relationship. You could always marry me and be a kept woman.'

Eva had thought a lot about that. Her motivation

to leave was receding the longer she knew Jed. And as the months passed she faced a dilemma. As much as she hated this town, Eva knew that she couldn't leave town if it meant leaving Jed Stephenson.

Chapter Ten

Eva

The shutters on the front of Jed's two-storey house banged as the cold westerly wind whistled around the house. Eva snuggled beneath the blanket on the sofa. 'You're going to have to go out and get more firewood soon, you know,' she said. The woodfire in the centre of the living room was burning low, but the room was still toasty warm.

'You reckon?' Jed pulled the blanket across to cover his legs.

'Yeah, and while you're up I thought you could put the kettle on and get that Dairy Milk chocolate out of the cupboard.' Eva chuckled as Jed stared at her. 'What?' she asked innocently.

'You don't care about the firewood, minx. You just want me at your beck and call.'

'Does beck and call include chocolate?' she asked with a cheeky grin.

Jed pushed the blanket off them and shivered when his bare feet hit the tiles. 'I'll get you chocolate if that's what you desire, my lady.'

Eva smiled as he walked out to the kitchen.

It was a cold Sunday afternoon in the middle of winter, and Jed and Evie were curled up under the blanket watching movies at Jed's house. It had taken a couple of months for Eva to realise that this amazing house up on the hill overlooking the small town and river actually belonged to Jed. He wasn't renting as she'd first assumed; he'd bought it as soon as he'd been appointed to the mine administration staff.

'I'm here to stay,' he said with a wide smile. 'I've got a great job. I love living in the country, and I've met this really sweet girl.' His eyes crinkled in that way she loved as he pulled her in for a kiss.

Over the months, as she'd fallen in love with Jed, she'd also fallen in love with his house. Very different to the ramshackle farmhouse where she and Zeke had grown up, this house was clean and modern, and the white shining tiles in every room on the bottom floor were exactly what Evie had always dreamed she would have in her house one day. Just as she'd dreamed of a fireplace like the huge circular one in his living room. Ever since she'd been about ten, it had been her job to sweep the ash from the two cold fireplaces in the farmhouse each morning before school. She'd hated doing it back then, but she did it for Jed, and it didn't bother her.

Evie had learned to hate the cold—and her farm life—as her stepfather had delegated more jobs to her as she entered her teens.

Chop the kindling, set the fire, feed the farm dogs.

'I'm bloody Cinderella,' she'd whinged to Mum the winter before Mum got sick.

'Language, please, Eva. We all have to pull our weight,' Mum had said with her tired smile. To be fair, Zeke did much of the farm work after school while Reg, their stepfather, had spent most of his time at the Royal Hotel. Things hadn't improved when Mum died, as Evie took over the cooking and the laundry at fourteen.

She'd hated cooking but now she was learning to enjoy it again as she cooked meals in Jed's kitchen. No scrimping and saving with the cheap cuts of meat and the seconds from the fruit and vegie bin out the back of the supermarket. Jed gave her access to his account at the local IGA and Eva loved shopping to fill his pantry.

Gradually she'd put some of her clothes and toiletries into his bedroom, but Jed still wouldn't let her move in.

He came back from the kitchen carrying a tray and the aroma of freshly-brewed coffee filled the room.

'Chocolate as requested. And coffee.' He put the tray on the low coffee table in front of the sofa.

'Thank you.'

Jed put his arm around her and pulled the blanket up and they settled back to watch the rest of the movie.

The chocolate didn't last long, and Eva snuggled back down beside Jed. Her attention wandered from the movie as thoughts filled her head. By the time the credits rolled, Eva had come to a decision.

Picking up the remote she pointed it at the huge television and turned it off. 'Jed?'

'Yes, my love?'

'Remember a couple of months ago you said you wouldn't let me move in, but I could always marry you and be a kept woman?'

He nodded. 'I do.'

'Was that a proposal?'

He leaned back on the sofa and his eyes were intent on hers. 'Why do you ask?'

'If it was, the answer is yes.'

The slow sweet smile that lit up his face was at

odds with the words that followed. 'Well, if that's why you want to know, no, it wasn't. No, it definitely wasn't a marriage proposal.'

Eva frowned when he jumped to his feet, and the chocolate wrapper and the blanket slid to the floor.

'Just stay there, and don't move. Promise?' he said. His voice was firm, and there was a strange expression on his face.

She nodded mutely, holding back the tears as disappointment knifed though her.

What a bloody stupid thing to say to him. You're a fool, Evangelina Asquith.

Jed left the room, and his footsteps pounded on the wooden steps as he ran upstairs. She looked around for her woolly socks and sneakers. It was time to go home.

No. Eva paused and stared at the blank television screen as she waited. She'd promised him she would stay.

Jed was back within seconds. He was holding something behind his back, and he held out his other hand and took hers as he kneeled beside the sofa.

'Now, my sweetest, lovely Evangelina, *this* is a proposal.' He moved his hand from behind his back and held out a beautiful ring that glowed blue in the dim light. 'Will you do me the honour of becoming my wife?' Jed's voice trembled as he held her gaze.

Eva's hand was shaking as she held it out, and tears ran down her face as Jed slipped the sapphire ring onto her left hand.

'Yes, Jed, I would love to be your wife.'

Chapter Eleven

Evie – Whitsundays

Evie lay on the deck with her eyes closed as *Kestrel* bobbed in the gentle swell. In her panic to get away from Jed and the island, she had sailed all afternoon and had foolishly left it until after dark to anchor in Queen Margrethe Bay on the eastern side of Shaw Island. It was usually one of her favourite anchorages, but the beauty of the water, and the small sliver of white sand of the narrow beach onshore glowing in the moonlight did nothing to take away the pain knifing through her.

She was beyond tears. Her stomach and her throat ached with the pain.

Plunging into the water and paying no heed to the danger of swimming across the bay to get to her boat had been driven by the need to get away from Jed; away from the emotions that he'd stirred within her with those few words he'd spoken.

Jed had tried to talk to her, but Evie knew if she listened to her husband and her brother, she would be trapped for her whole life. The only way to escape was to leave.

Seeing Jed on the path near the huts had shocked her at first. Her pulse had sped up and her muscles had quivered ready for flight, and anger had quickly followed.

How dare he come here? Pentecost Island, the first place in eight years where she had felt as though she truly belonged. A place where she knew she was valued and liked.

A place where she had formed friendships and where she knew the girls would look out for her.

Jed had tried to talk to her but when she'd turned away, he'd quickly realised that she wasn't going to stay and listen to him. So, he had told her simply in two cruel, brief sentences why he was there.

Confusion, grief, and despair had hit her like a physical shock, and Evie could barely remember anything else until she had pulled herself up into the boat. All she knew was she had to get away. Get away and process what he'd told her.

She opened her eyes and watched as the mast light swayed.

She wouldn't go back to Bylington.

Never.

She *couldn't*.

When Evie thought of what was at stake, she leaned forward and the pain at the back of her throat became too much and she finally gave into tears.

She would have to go back. Or to wherever Jed took her; she hadn't given him time to go into any detail. It wouldn't be Bylington, there was no hospital there.

Sitting up, she stared at the island to the west. There were no other boats in the bay, and no lights on the island. She was completely alone with only her grief to keep her company.

##

Evie slept out on the deck; she felt less confined there. Sleep came fitfully—she'd drift into a doze and then she'd think of what Jed had said, and then she would come awake with a jerk and more tears would come.

The early memories were sweet, and she lay there and let the happy times wash over her as she gave up trying to sleep. His news from home—told to her with no softening, and a demand that she came home, had bought their past back with a vengeance.

Sometimes, when she was trying to figure out what went wrong in her life, Evie blamed her aunt. If

Gloria hadn't decided to close the salon, maybe Evie would have stayed there, and she and Belinda could have made a go of it, and it would have given her something to fill her days.

But it wasn't the circumstances that had led her to make the decision that would change her life.

In her heart she knew that wasn't true. After she'd left Jed and Bylington, Evie had time to think about how she'd ended up the way she did.

The dark hateful words that she and Zeke had exchanged the day she told her brother she was leaving Jed, and Bylington, were imprinted on her soul.

'If you go, Eva, I will never speak to you again. Christ, woman, he *loves* you. How can you be so bloody cruel? You will be dead to me just like Mum is.'

She left and Zeke had never spoken to her again

Chapter Twelve

Eva - eight years ago

Circumstances and heightened emotions made for poor decisions. And Eva had made plenty of them in those few months. Poor Jed had tried his best. He would have given her anything she'd asked for.

They should never have married; she should have stuck to her original plan and left town.

Aunt Gloria had been so happy for her when Eva and Jed told the family they were getting married. And then she'd followed up her congratulations with, 'Good. Now I can close the salon.'

Even Reg had half-cracked a smile. Probably because he didn't have to be responsible for me anymore, Eva had thought.

'I can't afford to pay for any flash wedding,' was the first thing he'd said. Not, "I'm so happy for you" or "congratulations" or "welcome to the family, Jed". Reg's usual angst took the gloss off the happy announcement.

'It won't cost you a cent, Reg. We're having a quiet registry office wedding, aren't we, Jed?' Evie had put her arm through Jed's, but he'd looked down at her, surprised.

'Is that what you want? I thought every girl dreamed of a white wedding.'

'Eva's not every girl,' Reg had chipped in nastily.

Even Zeke had looked surprised at that low comment, but, as usual, he let it go. Zeke had always known what side his bread was buttered on. Mum had left the farm to her second husband, and Reg made the most of that.

Despite her family not being there—or maybe because they weren't—their wedding day had been beautiful. She and Jed picked a date, Belinda met them there, and one of Jed's mates from Brisbane had flown down to be his best man.

'That's a huge effort to make for one day,' Eva said when Jed had told her Boyd was coming to witness the wedding.

'That's what friends do,' he said. 'Are you really sure you don't want to have a big wedding and have all your friends there? And your family? Make it a celebration. I know you don't want to upset your stepfather, but I can afford to pay for a real wedding.'

'It will be a real wedding.' Eva shook her head and her words were emphatic. 'I don't have that many friends, and Reg isn't interested. It's our day, and Belinda's happy to be the other witness.'

'What about Zeke?' Jed asked.

'No. I want it to be *our* day.' Eva had said. She knew that Jed would fly to the moon and back if she'd asked him. She didn't want Zeke or her father there. She wanted the day to be theirs, and theirs alone, with no criticism or harsh words to spoil it.

And it had been a wonderful day.

It was a memory that Eva held in her heart and pulled out in later years when life was lonely. Jed had looked gorgeous in his dark suit, and she'd worn a short, fitted white dress, and a big hat. Belinda had done her hair and her makeup, and they'd met Jed and Boyd at the registry office in Dubbo.

When Jed looked at Eva as they stood waiting to be called in, the look in his eyes had turned her insides to a warm squishy jelly.

When the celebrant had said the words and they had repeated their vows, Eva had been filled with happiness.

For life.

Jed leaned over and his breath whispered on her cheek as his lips slid closer to hers. 'I love you.'

The next five minutes was a blur for Eva as the celebrant spoke and she and Jed responded, then the requisite paperwork was signed, and the marriage certificate was handed over.

'Don't forget to kiss your wife, mate,' Boyd said with a laugh. 'Again.'

Eva's happiness blossomed as Jed's arms went around her and his firm lips pressed against hers. A ripple of heat warmed her skin where his hand pressed into the small of her back. She looked up into his beautiful blue eyes and a shiver ran down her back.

Eva knew she'd never been as happy as she was in that moment. For the first time in her life, someone loved her enough to want to be with her, not only now, but to promise to be with her for a lifetime.

'I love you, Jed,' she said breathlessly when he finally lifted his head.

Belinda and Boyd chuckled when he kissed her for the third time and the sensation of Jed's lips pressing gently against hers set butterflies fluttering in Eva's tummy. She pressed her hand against his chest and pulled her head back to hold his gaze with hers. 'I love you very much.'

'Are we ready to go to the pub now?' Boyd asked. 'Or are you going to kiss your wife all afternoon?'

##

The afternoon had been filled with laughter as they celebrated their marriage. At one point, Eva's phone had buzzed, and her eyes had filled with happy tears when she read the text.

Hope you had a nice wedding, sis. xx

As much as it seemed strange to Jed, Zeke had understood why Eva didn't want them there.

Jed had looked at her and shaken his head. 'But he's your brother.'

'We're not a normal family, Jed. It's fine. And your family's not here, so it's only fair.'

He'd shrugged and hadn't raised it again.

Starting afresh with Jed was a chance for Eva to be happy and move on from the life she'd hated. There was no need to escape anymore; she'd found her escape in Jed. It wasn't the town that had caused her unhappiness; it had been her loneliness.

'Oh, Eva, he is so gorgeous,' Binny whispered in her ear when Jed and Boyd were at the bar ordering their drinks. 'And I'm so, so happy that you're not going to leave town.'

One miniscule niggle of regret rose, and Eva pushed it away. 'I'm happy too,' she said. 'I'm just sorry that Gloria closed up the salon and you haven't got a job now.'

'It's all good. I'm setting up at home. Dad's building a room on at the back of the garage. I'll still get all the clients. You can come and help if I get too busy.'

Eva shook her head. 'No way. A whole new life waits for me.'

What she hadn't expected was that, despite loving Jed, her new life hadn't been the escape she'd expected.

Tonight, lying alone on the deck of her boat, Evie wouldn't let herself think about how she felt seeing Jed Stephenson again. Even though she hadn't seen him since the last time he had tracked her down two years ago, her reaction to him was always the same.

The lines beside his eyes and his mouth had deepened in the last two years, but Evie refused to let herself be swayed by that. Jed was the one who had never wanted a divorce, and she'd told herself that didn't matter. She knew she wouldn't spend her life with him, and if he was happy to play the martyr, then that was his problem.

Her problem was that she still loved him, and she knew she always would.

Chapter Thirteen

Pippa

I put the phone down and shook my head. 'Evie's either got it switched off or is out of range,' I said to the girls. 'She'll be fine. And she'll come back.'

I hope.

We'd arranged to have our regular sunset girls' drinks this afternoon before the drama of the day had intervened. Eliza had come onshore from Phillipe's yacht, and Phillipe had gone up to chat to Rafe. Sienna and Nell had walked down from the house with Tam.

Without going into detail, I told them briefly that Evie had been upset about something and that she'd gone for a sail. I knew I could trust Tam not to say anything.

I stared out over the Passage wondering where Evie had fled to. The sky was purple with a storm threatening over the mainland, and a ragged cloud heading our way promised rain and wind later.

Rafe had suggested that we go out and look for her, but I'd disagreed. 'There are seventy-four islands out there with numerous bays and inlets, and you could search for days with no success,' I reminded him. 'And if you don't want to be found, there's all the cyclone moorings deep in the mangroves too.'

I pushed Evie from my thoughts. As much as I worried about her, she was an adult who could make her own choices. One thing I was going to do though, was see Jed Stephenson later and suggest to him that it wasn't worth staying.

Evie had told me that every couple of years, Jed would seek her out, check she was okay, and try to revive their marriage. That had surprised me; it was eight years since they'd split up.

I gave Jed points for persistence. He must really love her. It was a strange situation because I knew she cared for him.

'I can't stay long, gals.' Tam held up her glass as Nell popped the bottle of bubbles. 'I've got three dinner orders in tonight.'

Nell nodded. 'They've ordered ahead too. Each of the huts' guests have requested the three-meal-a-day option for the next week.'

'Excellent,' I said. 'Oh, and Tam, while I think of it, I rang Cherry Chilcott today.'

'And?' Tam raised her eyebrows. 'I hope she's a yes.'

'She's keen, but she can only work part-time for the first month. Does that suit you or would you rather advertise?'

Tam thought for a moment. 'That should be fine, as long as she's fulltime for at least a week or two before the wedding. She's a good worker, and she's had a lot of experience as a kitchen hand, both on Hamo and in Sydney. If you can chase up funding, I'd even offer her a traineeship.'

'As long as she's prepared to commit. We want to keep a settled staff.'

Sienna's laugh filled the night air and I looked across at her. As usual she was immaculately groomed in her silk pants and loose flowing top, and her hair was in its perfect bob. Nell and I were both wearing shorts and the resort T-shirt, and Tam was in her chef's uniform. Eliza was in a beach dress and had pulled her hair back into a neat ponytail, but Sienna always looked like she had stepped from the pages of a fashion magazine.

She spread her hands out gracefully and gestured around. 'Anyone who comes here falls under the spell of this island. I know I never want to leave.'

'Never?' Eliza said curiously. 'I thought you wanted to travel the world.'

Sienna shook her head. 'Once the day spa is built and up and running, this will be my world.' She turned to me with a smile. 'Pippa, I love it here, and I'm going to do my utmost to make the spa an exclusive establishment that will bring you guests from all over the world.'

'I like your style, Sienna,' I said as I took the glass that Nell handed me. 'Have you thought of a name for the spa yet? If you have, I can start doing some preliminary advertising material. I've had a look through the treatments that you listed, and I'm going to have the first appointment.'

'No, but I'm open to suggestions. And Pippa, the plans look fantastic. I love the idea of an open hut with views out to the water. It's going to be so relaxing! The mock-up the designer did is just what I imagined.'

'How about something classical, but with a beachy theme?' Nell said.

'That's what I was thinking, but every time I think of a name and look it up, there's already a spa with that name,' Sienna said. 'I imagine a Greek goddess type look with one of those gorgeous draping white dresses.'

She looked over towards the huts as someone stepped onto the path. 'Ooh, now that's the nicest looking man I've seen on the island. Shame all the guests here are couples.'

Tam and I looked at each other but neither of us mentioned that Jed wasn't part of a couple. I put my glass down on the rock. 'Keep thinking of names for Sienna's spa, gals. I just need to have a quick word to one of our guests. I'll be back in a while.'

I could hear them laughing behind me as names were suggested. I hoped it didn't turn into an argument like the one we'd had when we were naming the Turtle Bar. But we'd all been pretty stressed then, and I was reassured by the laughter that followed me up the beach.

'Pamper Palace,' Nell said with a giggle as I walked away.

'Paradise on Pentecost,' Eliza chipped in. 'Or Island Magic.'

'I was thinking Hebe,' Sienna said. 'She's the Greek goddess of youth and beauty.'

'He Be?' Tam chuckled. 'No, how about She Be?'

'Nope, it's a day spa for all, 'Sienna retorted. 'I had heaps of guys in for facials and skin work in

Switzerland.'

I smiled and kept walking, leaving them to it.

'Jed,' I called out when I was almost to the path. 'Can I have a quick word?'

He turned, and stood waiting for me to reach him, his expression curious, probably wondering how I knew his name. He didn't need to know that I had seen the photo on Evie's boat, so I recognised him straight away.

Their wedding photo.

I'd been surprised to see it there, but Evie had explained that she kept their photo to remind her how much she enjoyed her solitary life. Her excuse had never rung true to me. I was the only one on the island who knew about her past, and Evie talked about Jed a lot when we were alone.

She was kidding herself if she thought he didn't matter to her. I don't think she'd ever let him go. That's why I was curious about what had upset her so much. It didn't make sense.

'Hi,' I said holding out my hand. 'I'm Pippa Carmichael, one of the resort owners. I assumed you were Jed Stephenson because you came out of Serenity.'

'Serenity?' He frowned.

'Sorry, I mean Hut One. We've named the three huts but we're waiting for the signs to arrive.'

'Yes, I'm Jed.' He took my hand and shook it. 'Hello.'

Even though this guy had caused Evie a packet of grief, I did feel a bit sorry for him. He looked very tired and the shadows beneath his eyes were dark and deep. He lifted his head a little and his eyes narrowed as he looked at me. 'Hang on, are you the Pippa Carmichael Eva was friends with at uni?'

'I am.' I waited to see what his reaction would be and was surprised when his shoulders slumped.

'You probably wonder what I'm doing here.'

'The thought did cross my mind. It doesn't seem to be a holiday.'

'No.' His voice was quiet. 'It's certainly not that. Do you know where Eva is?'

I put my hand on his arm. 'Listen, how about you come up to the house with me and we'll have a coffee. There's no one there. I'd like to have a bit of a chat to you.'

He nodded and followed me up the path that led to the old house. Rafe and Phillipe were up at Rafe's house on the hill, and with the girls down on the beach, we'd have more privacy in the old house. I knew Tam would have left the coffee machine on, but as we headed along the path, I realised the time and I stopped walking. 'Actually, it's late. Let's go to the bar and have a drink.'

'A drink would be good.'

I changed direction and we walked over to the Turtle Bar. 'Beer? Wine? Spirits?' I offered when we walked inside and gestured to a table near the bar.

'A beer, thank you. Put it on my account.'

I waved my hand. 'No, count this as a welcome to the island.'

'Thank you.' He sat quietly as I poured a beer and then a glass of wine for me.

I sat down across from Jed and lifted my glass. 'Welcome to Pentecost Island.'

He clinked his glass against mine. 'Thank you.'

The silence was heavy as we both sipped, but Jed eventually broke it.

'I'm sorry I upset Eva. There was a bit of a scene.'

I nodded and didn't speak.

'I really have to talk to her. I've walked around the whole island and climbed the hills, but I've not seen her. I knocked on the door of the house, but there was no sign of anyone.'

'No, Nell usually mans the office and she's down on the beach with the girls.'

'And Eva. . .Evie?

'Evie's left the island, I'm afraid.'

Jed sat up straight and some of his beer sloshed on the table, but he didn't appear to notice. 'But I was watching the jetty. She didn't get on the boat when it dropped off those people before. I was watching from the hill behind the huts.'

'No,' I said slowly, wondering how much to say, but then I figured it wasn't a secret, and I didn't know exactly where Evie was anyway. 'She left on her boat.'

'Shit. I'd forgotten about her boat. How the hell could I have forgotten that?' Jed said half to himself. He reached up with one hand and rubbed his forehead. 'She does work here though, doesn't she? I thought she lived on the island. Will she come back or have I frightened her off?'

He looked so forlorn my heart went out to him. 'Jed? I'm going to be honest with you. I know about your past with Evie . . . or Eva . . . as you call her. I'm sorry to hear that you upset her, because, and again I'll be honest, I know she cares about you. I'm the only one here who knows you were married, and she does speak to me about you sometimes. There's no ill will.'

'I know there's not.' The sadness in his voice was heartbreaking. He lifted his head and his eyes were clouded. 'I came to see her about something else and that's why she got so upset. It was a shock to her. I need her to come home with me.'

'I guess that's up to Evie,' I said.

'How long do you think it will be before she comes back?' Jed asked. 'I've booked the hut for a week because I know Eva . . . Evie. I know it's going to take a bit of persuading to get her home, but I know she'll agree in the end. She'll do the right thing.'

'You seem very confident.' I frowned. 'She might stay away for a week or more.'

'Do you have her mobile number? Or can you get in touch with her boat by radio?'

'You know her well enough, I guess. If she doesn't want to talk to anyone, we won't be able to contact her. But I'm sure she'll be back soon. My partner and I are getting married in six weeks, and I know she'll come back because she's in charge of our grounds. Evie won't let us down.'

'We need her in Brisbane now. She won't be

able to stay here for six weeks.'

I'd heard a lot about Jed over the years, but not once had Evie ever said he was selfish or demanding. 'Really?'

Chapter Fourteen

Eva - eight years earlier

'Jed?'

Eva's husband of eleven months was sitting at the dining room table, his laptop opened in front of him, and scheduling sheets spread over the table. It was the only part of their two-storey house that wasn't perfect; thanks to the cleaning service the tiled floors gleamed white, the kitchen was scrubbed clean, the washing was done and folded away, and Jed's business shirts were ironed for the two weeks ahead.

'Yes, babe,' he said absently without taking his eyes from the screen. But he did reach up and take her hand when she walked across to stand behind him. He looked tired and his glasses were pushed back above his forehead and his hair was standing on end.

Eva smoothed his hair flat with her free hand. 'I've been thinking.'

'A dangerous occupation,' he said with a smile.

'Will you be serious?' she said shortly. 'Please?' The last word held a note of apology.

Jed was always happy, and ready to

accommodate anything Eva wanted. Even though it was the opposite to the household she had left where she had been at the beck and call of her stepfather and brother, Eva sometimes found it hard to cope with Jed's constant and even disposition.

A month after their wedding he'd been promoted at the mine, and to her dismay, the new position meant time away from home. Over the past few months Jed had been away at least two to three nights each week. One thing she'd not realised before they'd married was his focus on his career and his intense determination and drive to get to the top.

Since his promotion, most nights when he *was* at home with Eva were spent on work. At first, he'd worked in his study, but with his usual empathy, Jed had sensed that she was lonely, and now he worked at the table in the dining room adjacent to the kitchen.

Now Eva rattled around in the house; there was little for her to do as Jed had insisted on retaining the cleaning service and he kept on a local woman he'd hired to attend to the laundry and ironing. Eva baked and prepared so many meals in advance, the two freezers were full.

Her busy life at Gloria's salon had come to a

sudden end when the doors had closed the week before the wedding, and Zeke had swung some fairly heavy hints about her helping out at the farm.

You could only read so many books in a week, and keep the gardens weeded, she thought to herself, before she had her brainwave. The last three months she'd taken a lot of pleasure creating a permaculture garden around the house and Jed had told her how good it was looking, even with the drought.

'So, what have you been thinking, love?'

'I . . . um . . . I'm a bit nervous.'

Jed frowned and took his glasses off before he slid the chair back. He pulled her down onto his lap and put his arms around her. 'Please, don't ever feel that way. I don't want us to be like that. I want you to know you can say anything to me. We have to be honest with each other about everything, Eva.'

She nodded and bit her lip.

'Have I done something to upset you?' he asked pulling her closer. 'Are you bothered by me being away?'

'No. Well, maybe a little, but that's not what I want to talk to you about. I just want to ask you something. Something that I really want to do.'

'Anything you want. Just ask. I will buy you anything your heart desires.' He leaned back and his eyes widened before he smiled at her. 'Unless, it's something money won't buy? You want to have a baby?'

Eva pulled a face. 'God, no. I'm only twenty.'

'Good. I'm not ready for children. Yet. I want us to have some time for ourselves before we start a family.'

'Yes. I agree.'

'So?' He tipped his head to the side. 'What do you want to ask me?'

'It's not something I want to have. It's something I want to do.'

Jed gently took her chin in his hand and looked at her. 'Eva, I am not in charge here. We have a partnership. If you want to do something you don't have to ask my permission.'

Her eyes pricked with tears. 'I guess I'm used to having to ask permission for anything I wanted.'

'Well, no more. If you're happy, I'm happy. Now tell me what you want, love.'

She swallowed, still nervous, no matter how supportive Jed was. 'Well, you know how you're away a fair bit since you got the promotion?'

He nodded.

'And you know how much I'm enjoying the garden?'

'I do. And you are doing an amazing job of it.' Jed smoothed her hair away from her eyes.

She rushed on. 'I've been looking at courses, and there's one in Brisbane I'd really love to do.'

'Go for it. We can afford for you to fly there and stay there. How long does it go for?'

'Well, that's the thing you see.'

'The thing?'

'It's a degree course. I'd have to go up and stay there during the term time.' Eva felt Jed tense, but his expression still held a smile.

'If that's what you want, we can work it out.' He dropped his chin onto the top of her head. 'I know how lonely you've been the last few months with me away, Eva. And you've not once complained. It's not your sole job in life to make me happy. I want you to be happy too.'

Relief shuddered through her. 'Really? You don't mind if I go away and study?'

'I'll miss you, but of course I'll manage. I can

come and see you and you can come home some weekends. And uni only goes from March to October, so it's not as though you'll be gone for three solid years.'

Eva reached up and put her arms around Jed's neck. 'You will never know in a million years how much I love you.'

Chapter Fifteen

Evie – the Whitsundays

They hadn't had a million years for Jed to know that. Before another year had passed Eva had left Bylington . . . and her marriage. Circumstances had changed for both of them, and Eva's emotional response to those circumstances had strengthened her need to escape.

Circumstances. Emotions. Decisions.

Jed had gone to the United States on a three month study course on mine machinery during Eva's second semester at university and Grandpa had turned up in Brisbane in his boat a week after she'd seen Jed off at Brisbane airport.

Jed had held her close and she'd buried her face into his shoulder.

'I'm going to miss you so much, Eva.'

'You be careful over there,' she said into his shirt. 'Don't go out at night and be careful driving on those freeways. I'll worry about you every minute you're gone.'

'I will. And you be careful here. Study hard, and

the time will fly. I'll ring you every night once I work out the time difference.'

But Jed had been busy, and the calls had not been as frequent as he'd planned. They'd seemed to grow apart since Eva had started her course.

Or since he'd taken the promotion, she thought.

Circumstances changed more when Grandpa sailed into Moreton Bay.

##

Late the next afternoon, Evie lowered the mainsail as *Kestrel* approached the front bay at Pentecost Island. The sun was hovering above the mainland and the sky was shot with the usual evening magnificence. Ragged purple streaks edged the burnt orange clouds to the west, and the wind dropped off as night fell. A group of seabirds had followed her all the way from Shaw Island, and Evie lifted a hand and bid them farewell as they kept heading east once she turned her boat into the bay.

She had come to a decision last night; running away was not the right course of action. She had done that once before and look how she'd ended up.

Alone . . . and lonely.

Until she'd come to this island.

Evie wasn't keen on going south with Jed, but if she could make a difference, she *would* go. If it hadn't been so important, Jed wouldn't have come.

The grounds had to be prepared for Pippa and Rafe's wedding and she was determined to have them perfect. It wasn't a good time for her to go away, but Evie knew she would go with Jed. She had no choice.

Evie knew she owed Pippa; she had been a close friend in the six months Evie had stayed in the uni course, and Pippa had spent many nights listening to her outpourings as Evie had pondered her future.

'I love Jed,' she had said one night as they sat on the back veranda of the old Queenslander that Pippa shared with Tamsin and Nell in those uni days. Tam and Nell both worked part-time at night, and Evie didn't know them very well. 'But the thought of going back to Bylington, and to the house and my life there makes me physically ill.'

'Have you told Jed how you feel? The feeling sick part, I mean?' Pippa leaned back on the old ratty sofa and her gaze was intent on Evie.

She shook her head. 'How can you tell the person you love that the thought of being with him makes you feel sick. It's not Jed, Pip. It's the place.'

'What's so bad about the "place"?'

Evie had stared down the hill as she tried to find the right words. A large sports oval was at the bottom of the street and a couple of teams were kicking a soccer ball around under the bright lights.

'Every bad thing that has ever happened to me happened in that town. My dad was killed in a farm accident when I was a baby. I don't even remember him. Mum married my stepfather when I was seven and I know how unhappy she was with Reg. Then she died, and I had to cook and clean and look after him and my brother. Then I got a hairdressing apprenticeship and I hated that. The town is a horrid place. It's always held bad memories for me, and I feel trapped. Then Jed turned up, and I lost sight of the bad things for a while. I should never have married him.'

'But you love him?'

'I do, and the thought of making him unhappy makes me feel sick too.'

'Would Jed move?'

'He would have.' Evie had shaken her head. 'But I wouldn't ask him to. His career is important to him, and he wants to get to the top. If I asked him to move, I know he would—in a heartbeat—but eventually he would resent me for that.'

'It sounds to me like you've made a decision already, Evie.' Pippa's voice was sad. To her credit, she had not endorsed or criticised Evie's decision at all, but she had listened with a sympathetic ear.

'If you need to talk, I'll always be here for you.'

And Pippa had been, and when they'd bumped into each other on Hamilton Island eight years later, and Pippa had offered Evie the job on Pentecost Island, she had been content.

So now she would pay Pippa back for her friendship, and she would do the right thing by her brother. She would do both, no matter what it took. Or how hard it was.

Zeke was her only living relative. No matter what he had said to her the day she'd left Bylington—and Jed—and no matter that she hadn't seen or spoken to her brother for almost eight years, Zeke was her brother and if she could help him, she would.

Evie sighed as the motor started and she turned the wheel to port. She and Zeke had had a difficult relationship in their teens. When Mum had died, he had gone through a wild stage; even though he'd only been sixteen, he'd gone out drinking most nights, and the worst part of it was that their stepfather could see nothing wrong with that.

'It doesn't hurt the boy to have a couple of drinks. He works hard, he's almost a man,' Reg had yelled at her one night when she'd tried to stop Zeke going to town with the single motive of getting drunk.

Evie had never been intimidated by Reg. 'He is underage, and like you just said, he is a boy,' she'd yelled back.

She'd copped a backhander for that, but her stepfather was a crafty man; no-one ever saw him hit her. The same as Mum; the bruises she'd had had all been explained away as clumsiness.

But if getting drunk was Zeke's way of coping, Evie's was to go inside herself and block out the world around her. Sometimes she could even pretend that Mum was at the farm waiting for her to get home from high school.

But Mum hadn't been. She was in the cemetery on the other side of town, and all the pretending in the world couldn't make things better.

Zeke had understood Evie—and her need to be by herself. He'd understood why she'd shut down, as he'd understood why she wanted a quiet wedding. He'd pulled back on the drinking when he'd started working at the mine. Zeke and Jed had become good mates and Evie knew that he had seen Jed as a positive role model.

The only thing he'd not been able to understand was why Evie had to leave.

When Evie and Jed were first married, Zeke and Sam had come over for dinner once a month, and even though she had nothing in common with Zeke's new wife, Evie had made an effort.

There had been a fragile peace between the siblings, until the day Eva told Zeke she was leaving.

It was only minutes before she turned *Kestrel* into the channel. Evie pulled a face. Changing the boat name obviously hadn't worked; Jed had found her again.

But this time she could understand why. Knowing Jed, he would have searched to the ends of the earth until he found her.

With a deep breath she focused on her boat and as she steered her into the channel between the coral heads, a small welcoming committee had gathered on the jetty.

Pippa and Tamsin were standing at the beach end near the steps that led up to Rafe's house. There was no sign of Jed, but Evie had no doubt that he would still be on the island. He would have won everyone over with his natural charm, and he would wait here until she returned.

To be fair, he was genuine and a good man; she just hadn't been good enough for him.

Pippa was waiting for Evie to throw the rope. She caught it deftly and secured *Kestrel* to the bollards on the jetty.

Evie pushed her hands through her hair and took a deep breath as she climbed over the side to a reception she wasn't expecting.

Tam's eyes were flashing, and her hands were on her hips. 'Don't you ever, ever do that to me again, Evie!'

Evie had forgotten that she'd heard Tam running after her, but she'd been focused on getting to her boat.

She held Tam's gaze steadily. 'I'm sorry. I was a bit out of it. I didn't give a thought to the danger of swimming across the bay. I heard you calling me, but—'

Tam reached out and hugged her. 'I thought you'd been taken by a shark.'

'Well, I wasn't. But I promise I won't do it again. I was just trying to get away.' She looked towards

Pippa and then to the huts. 'Is Jed still here?'

Pippa reached out and hugged her too. 'Welcome home. And yes, he is. Is that okay?'

Evie nodded. 'Yes, I knew he would be. I'll talk to him later. Where is he?'

'I think he was heading over to the bar. He's ordered his dinner to be delivered there,' Tam said.

'Anyone else ordered dinner to eat over there?'

'The other two huts are eating in. So, it's only Jed.'

Evie swallowed. 'How long until his meal is ready?'

'Another hour,' Tam said.

'Okay. If it's all right with you I'll take the tray down to the bar, and talk to him then.' Evie didn't miss the satisfied look that Tam and Pippa exchanged. 'Did Jed tell you exactly why he was here?' she asked.

Pippa shook her head. 'No.'

'Okay. Good.' Evie kept her voice firm. If she thought about what was looming, she'd let stress take over, and she wasn't going to do that again. Not in front of the girls or in front of Jed. 'I'll go back to the house and have a shower and I'll meet you in the kitchen in a while. Okay, Tam?'

'All good.' Tam hugged her again briefly before she walked off the jetty. 'You take care, girlfriend. We've all got your back, you know.'

That was enough to make Evie choke up, but she kept the tears and the shaky voice at bay. 'Thank you. You don't know what it means to have friends who care about me.'

It was Pippa's turn to hug. 'Oh, we do that Evie. All for one, and one for all here.'

Chapter Sixteen

Evie

Evie had a small room at the back of the original house at Ma Carmichael's and shared a bathroom with the other girls. The two dresses she'd bought at Hamo when she'd gone over with Sienna and Tam three weeks ago hung in the alcove in the corner. After a quick shower, she slipped the bright yellow one over her head, and picked up the chunky brown beads that were hanging on the brass hook on the old hall stand she used as a dressing table.

Sienna knocked on the door as Evie stood there trying to figure out what to do with her hair.

'Want some company, Evie?' Her lilting voice called though the half-open door.

'Come in, Sienna.'

Sienna walked in and nodded as she looked at Evie 'You look very nice.'

'Thank you. I've got to have a conversation with someone and it's going to be tough. I thought getting dressed up might help, but it's not.'

Sienna frowned. 'Can I ask who?'

Evie pulled a face. 'My ex-husband. Well technically my husband. We never divorced.'

Sienna's mouth dropped open. 'Oh. And of course, you want to look your best. Stay right there.'

She was back in seconds with her makeup suitcase. Putting it on the bed, she dragged the small stool from beneath the window over to the hall stand. 'Sit there. Are you going to dry your hair?'

'I don't have time.'

Sienna nodded, stood behind her and picked up the wide-toothed comb. 'Don't argue. I can have you ready and gorgeous in five minutes.'

She combed Evie's hair back and then twisted it into a tight bun on the back of her head.

'You have the most beautiful bone structure, Evie. With your high cheekbones, and your almond-shaped eyes, you need very little work. Just a touch of colour on your lids to match your green eyes, and some pale lip gloss, and you are perfect.' Her expression was knowing. 'That way you don't look as though you have tried to look beautiful, which I am guessing is how you want to appear.'

Evie reached back and squeezed Sienna's hand.

'You are guessing right. And thank you for being such a good friend.'

'It's what I love about being here. Eliza has always been a good friend to me, but since I've met you girls on the island, I really value your friendships too. I've never felt supported as much as I do here.'

'They're a pretty special bunch of women, that's for sure.'

'And you're a part of that too. Don't you ever doubt that, Evie. If you need a friend after your conversation, I'll be here on the veranda.'

'I probably will.' Evie forced a chuckle. 'Have a bottle of wine open!'

Her stomach was churning as she slipped on a pair of sandals and headed to the kitchen.

Tam had a tray ready, and there were two stainless steel dish covers covering the plates.

'I did a meal for you too, Evie. There's nothing worse than trying to talk when one person is eating. It's only curry and rice.'

'Thank you.' Before Evie picked up the tray, she walked over and hugged Tam. 'And thank you for being my friend. This is all very new to me. I've never really had girlfriends before.'

Tam's cheeks flushed and she hugged Evie back. 'I'll be here for you if you need some company when you come back.'

This time it was easier to smile. 'Sienna's going to be waiting on the veranda with a bottle of wine.'

Tam grinned. 'Okay, and I'll bring dessert.'

'I like that idea.' Evie smiled back as she lifted the tray. 'I could be a while. I have a lot of questions for Jed and some arrangements to make. I'll tell you about it later. Maybe see if Pippa and Eliza and Nell can join us. I might as well tell you all at once.'

As she walked down to the bar, Evie tried to clear her mind by focusing on the gardens and paths and cataloguing what she would need to do before the wedding.

When she saw the area that had been pegged out for the new restaurant, she knew she needed to get everything else done first, because the landscaping around the new building would take at least ten days to complete. She was going to have to see Pippa and hire a couple of labourers; if she had more time, she could have done the work herself, but time was an unknown factor at the moment. It would all depend on how long she'd be away.

She knew she was going to have to be firm with Jed, but she guessed that was out of his control too.

By the time she approached the bar, she had herself under control. Jed was facing the water and he didn't hear her approach; her leather sandals were quiet on the pavers.

She slid the tray onto the table and Jed turned around.

'Thank—' His mouth dropped open and he stared at her.' Eva!'

'Hello, Jed. I'm back.'

'Yes . . . Evie.' He nodded, and his knuckles were white where his hand gripped the back of the chair. 'I can see that.'

'Please sit down. Your dinner will be getting cold.'

'I'm not really hungry.' His voice was soft, but as deep and smooth as ever, and still sent a shiver down Evie's spine.

'Well, I am,' she said briskly, ignoring the shaky feeling in her legs as she met her husband's eyes. 'Sit down and we'll eat while we talk. I don't have much time. I have a . . . um . . . a work meeting after I talk to you.'

He waited until she sat down and then he sat, not once taking his eyes off her.

Evie fought to keep her composure, but it was hard. She pushed the tray to the middle of the table and picked up one of the napkins rolled around the cutlery and put it in front of Jed's place setting. She kept her eyes down as she removed the two meals from the tray, lifted the lids and placed them back on the tray. She slid one of the bowls of curry towards him and pulled the other towards her. The aroma of the fragrant curry and jasmine rice made her stomach churn more than it already was.

'Thank you.' Jed unrolled the napkin and placed the knife onto the table. He twirled the fork in his fingers and looked down at the meal.

'Dig in,' Evie said with false brightness in her voice, 'and then we'll talk.' She picked up her fork and moved a few grains of rice from one side of the bowl to the other. 'Oh look, Tam has some pappadams in that packet.' She reached for the packet in the middle of the tray, but her hand stilled when Jed dropped his fork with a clatter.

'For God's sake, Eva. Stop it. Just stop it.' Jed's voice broke and he put his hand across his eyes. 'We can be civilised without all this false social shit. Can't we? Please?'

It was the first time Jed had ever sworn at her, and Evie's throat closed. She dropped her head and stared down at the bright yellow butter curry. 'It's my way of coping, Jed. I'm sorry I ran from you the other day. I should have stayed to listen then, but I couldn't. I just couldn't. Not when you told me why you were here.'

She watched as Jed reached across the table and took her hand in his. The nerve endings through her whole body fired in response to his touch.

'I know and I'm sorry I was so blunt, but I could see you weren't willing to talk to me. I'm sorry I was so harsh with you, but it was the only way. The only way to make you listen before you walked away again.'

Evie squeezed his fingers before removing her hand from his warm clasp. 'It's all right. I've had time to process what you said. Tell me how long Zeke has been sick and what I need to do.'

Chapter Seventeen

Jed

Jed found if he ate while he talked, that Eva, Evie—he had to get used to that name—would eat too, and it seemed to help both of them keep calm.

'Zeke first got sick about eighteen months ago. He was diagnosed with an aggressive blood cancer, but the initial treatment was successful. He had a stem cell transplant and went into remission.'

'Why didn't someone tell me?' Evie's eyes were sad as she stared at him.

'I couldn't find you. I tried, Evie. It was hard because when I mentioned it to Zeke, he said he didn't want you to know, but I thought you should. In the end it didn't matter, because I couldn't find you and he responded to the treatment. We thought he'd won his fight. He started to work on the farm again and I went home.'

'I was in Vanuatu,' she said. 'I sailed over there and spent three months working in a volunteer group to help them re-establish their agricultural plots on one of the smaller islands after the cyclone.'

Jed paused as he lifted his fork. 'By yourself? In *Eros*?'

'Yes, by myself. In *Kestrel*. I've changed the name of Grandpa's boat.'

'You changed it so I couldn't find you again?'

'No. Maybe.' Evie shrugged and wouldn't meet his eyes. 'I don't know. I never liked the name anyway. Keep telling me about Zeke.' She lifted her head and looked at him again. 'And what did you mean about going home?'

'I helped out on the farm when he was in hospital. He got sick again a month ago, and when he told me that the prognosis wasn't too good this time, I was determined to find you.' Jed put his fork down. As tasty as the curry was, it was sticking in his throat. He reached for the glass of water he'd filled from the water cooler on the bar before Evie had arrived. He took a moment to gather his thoughts. Nothing had changed; she obviously found his company difficult.

'I knew you'd been on Hamilton Island for a while, so I made some enquiries, and someone said they thought that you were working over here on Pentecost Island. I flew straight up here from Brisbane and I didn't even know if you were here, or not until I saw you on the path over there yesterday. And once I knew you were here, I wasn't leaving until I talked to you.'

Looking at Evie was hard.

No matter how hard she pushed him away, or how obvious it was she didn't want to be in his presence, Jed couldn't stop how he felt about her, any more than he could will his heart to stop beating. He had loved Evangelina Asquith from the first moment he'd met her, and it had almost broken him when she'd left.

She'd never loved him enough; Jed knew that now. He had been a way for Eva to escape her family and her past.

He swallowed. 'I had to talk to you. You may be Zeke's last chance.'

'Me? I could?' She looked at him again and her forehead wrinkled in a frown. 'You said he was dying. And that I need to see him.'

'And then you took off before I could tell you why I was here.'

'And?'

Jed took a deep breath. Everything hinged on her response. Zeke's chances of surviving, his future.

This was why he was here, and without Zeke's

knowledge. He and Evie's brother had been close over the past few years. Zeke always said he would never forgive Evie for leaving, but he had stayed a good mate to Jed, and supported Jed as he'd learned how to cope without her in his life. Zeke had been the one who had made him realise that the long hours he was working at the mine were his way of dealing with his marriage breakup, and that he had no life.

Jed gathered his thoughts before he spoke. 'Zeke has one chance. A bone marrow transplant. The doctors agree if they can find a match, he has an excellent chance of a full recovery.'

'How do they find a match?'

'On the international bone marrow register; it's not looking good. There was no match.' Jed looked at his wife as he carefully chose his words. 'The other likely match is through a sibling. You are your brother's last chance of surviving. The odds are good. There's a one in four chance that you will be a perfect match.'

She nodded slowly. 'What do I need to do?'

'You're willing to help?'

'Of course I am, Jed.' Despite her words, Evie's voice was sad. 'What do you think I am? Heartless? No matter what's happened between you and me, Zeke is my brother and I'll do whatever it takes to help him.'

'Thank you.' He let out the breath he'd been holding. 'There's only one more thing I need to tell you. I didn't tell Zeke I was looking for you.'

'We'll sort that out when I get there. If he can be bloody-minded about this, so can I. If I *am* a match, I'll do what it takes. If not, I'll make my peace with my brother and I'll help him fight.' Evie's voice trembled and it was all Jed could do not to reach out to her. 'I asked you what I need to do.'

'The first step is as simple as a cheek swab. The doctors match donors to patients based on their human leukocyte antigen tissue type. They're proteins, found on most cells in your body. Your—'

'Forget all that. Just tell me how I do it.'

'Zeke and Sam and the boys are in Brisbane. They used to stay at my place when he came up for monthly treatment, but this time Sam and the boys are in a cottage at the hospital. Zeke's oncologist is a top Brisbane specialist.'

The colour leached from Evie's cheeks.

'Boys? What boys?'

'Zeke and Sam have two boys. Jimmy is five and Liam is two.'

The cry from her lips almost broke his heart. 'I didn't know. Why didn't you tell me when you saw me two years ago?'

Jed's words were harsher than he intended. 'Because you made it quite clear you didn't want to have anything to do with me. If I recall correctly, we spoke for about five minutes and that was mainly you telling me to leave you alone.'

'I'm sorry, I wasn't in a good place then.'

Jed bit back his words. He felt like saying he hadn't been in a good place since she'd left him in Bylington eight years ago. 'Let's not argue. We need to make some plans.'

She nodded without speaking.

'It would be better if you came to Brisbane as soon as you can. You won't have trouble taking time off?'

'No,' she replied quietly.

'If you're a match, it's a simple procedure in hospital, and then you'll be right to go. I'll book us on the first flight I can from Hamilton Island.'

Again, a nod, before Evie spoke. 'Just one question, Jed?'

'Yes?'

'What do you mean your place in Brisbane?'

He shrugged. 'Just what I said. My place. I moved back into the family house at the Bay when my parents passed away. That's where I live now. You can stay there if you're happy to. I have a guest suite.'

'Did you get your promotion?'

It was the first time Evie had shown any sort of interest in his life since she'd left him. Jed had struggled for a long time, and the decision he had finally made had been the right one for him. He'd settled into his new life and had managed to get over Evie.

Or he thought he had until he'd seen her yesterday. No matter how long it had been, his heart still leapt, and he knew he would never stop loving her. Maybe if they divorced, it would be easier for him to get over her.

Chapter Eighteen

Eva - eight years earlier

'I can't believe you're in Brisbane the same time as me, Grandpa!' Eva hugged her grandfather and closed her eyes as the familiar comforting smell of hair cream and the rub of rough whiskers on her cheek took her back to her childhood. She'd come down to the marina at Manly on Moreton Bay where he'd moored *Eros*.

She'd been surprised, but very pleased to get a phone call from him, although Grandpa had originally called to let her know that he was on his way to visit Bylington.

'It's worked out very well. It's going to save me a trip down there. I'll give Zeke a ring though.' Grandpa held her at arm's length. 'You look good, sweetheart.' He reached up and flicked a finger on her hair. 'I'm pleased to see your hair is back to its natural colour. You're looking more like your grandmother— God rest her soul—every day.'

'I'm not in hairdressing anymore, so I don't have to try out all the products and colours.'

'I'm very pleased to hear that. So, what are you

doing in Brisbane?'

'I'm at university. I'm studying landscape architecture.'

'So that tight-arsed bugger your mother stupidly married finally paid your way, did he? Or did you save up?'

'Reg died three months ago.'

'No loss. loathed that slimy bugger. So, Zeke's got the farm and your share helped you get to uni?'

'Yes and no. Zeke's working the farm, yes. He left the mine.' Eva smiled at him and held out her left hand. 'My husband's helping me pay for uni.'

'What the . . .? You're married and you didn't invite me to the wedding! I'll be buggered! When did that happen?'

'Last year, but I thought you were up in the islands. I tried to ring you for weeks, and there was no answer. I stopped worrying when I got that postcard from Broome. You really need to keep in touch more.'

Grandpa shook his head. 'You and Zeke are grown up now. You have your own lives. I have mine, and we catch up when we can. Family ties bind tight, love, no matter where we are, or how long between visits. Now, come and sit out on the deck, and tell me all about this husband of yours, and then I'll tell you my news.'

Grandpa made coffee while she waited on the deck. Closing her eyes, Eva listened as he rattled around in the galley. The air was damp and salty, and she relaxed, absorbing the smells and sounds of the sea. Gulls squawked overhead, and the occasional hoot of the ferry horn across the bay were the only sounds apart from the soothing slap of the small waves on the side of the hull.

This was her happy place. Suddenly, the thought of going back to Bylington cut though her like a knife. Her eyes flew open, and she frowned. Jed was in Bylington—that should be enough to make her keen to return. There was only two weeks of the semester left and then after her exams, he would come back from the States and they would be home together for four months.

'Here you go.' Her grandfather put his coffee on the deck and opened out a small folding stool. He sat down slowly and awkwardly, and Eva frowned.

'Are you okay, Grandpa? You look a bit stiff there.'

'My arthritis is playing up, love. I've had to come to a decision. As much as I hate the thought, I'm going to become a landlubber. That's what I wanted to talk to you about, but you being married and at university has put a spanner in the works.'

'In what way?'

He lifted his coffee cup and looked at her over the rim. 'I'm giving you *Eros.*'

'But . . . but where will you live?'

'I've bought myself a little unit in a retirement facility two streets away.' He gestured to the western side of the marina. 'Close enough to walk down to the water, and close enough to smell the sea every day.' He grinned at her and the weathered skin around his pale blue eyes crinkled. 'And now you're living in Brissie, you can use the boat whenever you want—your boat— and maybe take your old Grandpa out for a sail some days.'

Evie bit her lip. 'I—we—don't live in Brisbane.'

Grandpa frowned. 'Where do you live?'

Eva knew her voice was strained. 'Still in Bylington. Jed, my husband, is the assistant manager at the new coal mine.'

'Ah.' His gaze was shrewd. 'So, you didn't escape that town after all?'

'No, but I escaped Reg and the farm, and Jed

and I live in a lovely house on the hill, but yes, I'm still there. He's away a lot and I come to uni for two semesters each year.'

'I'm sorry, I might be old-fashioned, but that doesn't sound like much of a relationship to me. These modern days.' He shook his head. 'When your Gran and I were married, the only time we were apart was the week she was in hospital when your mother was born.' Grandpa held her eyes for a long time, and finally she looked away.

'Is that what you want?' he asked.

'Half and half. I love Jed. He's a wonderful guy, but I still hate living in Bylington. I don't know what I want, Grandpa.' She put one hand over her eyes as tears threatened. 'But I do. I want Jed, but not in Bylington.'

'Would your husband move?'

Eva shook her head. 'I wouldn't ask him to. He's working towards a promotion, and that's the best place for him to do it.'

'And will you be happy when he gets that promotion?'

'I'll be happy for him.'

'But what about you, love? All your dreams? It looks to me as though you've given a lot of them away.

Are you enjoying university?'

Eva thought as she sipped her coffee. 'It's not what I expected. To be honest, I guess I've been thinking about whether I even want to come back next semester. But the thought of being back in Bylington with nothing to do when Jed's away makes me ill. I've made a few friends here and that's been good for me. Most of the girls I knew at high school have moved away to Dubbo or Sydney.'

'Well, sweetheart. It sounds like you have some decisions to make. Whatever you decide, *Eros* is yours. You don't have to wait until I kick the bucket. I know you'll love her and look after her.

'But what about Zeke? You can't give her to me. That wouldn't be fair.'

'Did Zeke give you a payout for your share of the farm?'

'No. I didn't need it.'

'You were entitled to it. Your mother and father worked hard to build that property up. I tried to talk her into selling when your father was killed, but she was stubborn.' He chuckled. 'Like her old man, and like her daughter too, I think. Okay, Zeke has the farm, you get the boat. That's fair to me.'

Eva put her cup on the deck and stood. She walked over to the stool and kneeled beside it. She leaned into her grandfather's shoulder and her voice was muffled. 'I miss Mum so much, Pa.'

His weathered hand stroked her hair. 'I know, sweetheart. Life's hard.' He reached down and tilted her chin up so that she was looking at him. 'One thing I want you to always remember. Life is hard, but life is *short*. So, don't waste any time doing things you don't want to do. It's not selfish, but you need to think carefully about what you want in life, and whether the partner you choose wants the same things that you do.'

She nodded. 'I will.'

'And whatever you decide, *Eros* is yours. I've taken out a ninety-nine year lease on this berth. It's all paid up. She just needs someone to look after her.'

Chapter Nineteen

Eva – eight years earlier

Going back to Bylington was going to be hard, more so after four months away. Before he'd gone overseas, Jed had come up for two weekends while Eva had been in Brisbane, and they'd stayed at a posh hotel in the city each time. He was supposed to fly into Brisbane and pick her up after her final examination next week but had called last night.

'Eva, sweetie, I'm so sorry. I have to fly to Western Australia for two weeks on the way back from here. I'll book a flight to Dubbo for you and get Zeke to pick you up. Or even better, why don't you look for a car to buy in Brisbane and take your time driving home. When you find one, let me know and I'll transfer the money across to your account.'

'No, it's okay. I'll stay up here and do some work until you get home. You can come up then.' Eva didn't say that the work she was doing would be on *Eros*, not her uni work. For some reason—and she couldn't figure out why—she hadn't mentioned *Eros* or Grandpa to Jed yet. She'd told herself that she wanted it to be a surprise when she took Jed there when he came over, and they could have a weekend on the water, but she wondered if she wasn't being entirely honest with herself.

Eros was hers, and Eva was enjoying the time she spent on her. It was *her* time, and *her* boat, and she hugged that close; she made a conscious decision not to examine why she felt like that.

Jed had been trying to talk her into buying a car to use in Brisbane, but Eva was quite happy living in a residential hall at the uni and using public transport to get around. Since Grandpa had come back and settled into his new apartment, she'd spent most weekends on *Eros*. There was a bus from the city out to the Bay, and some days, she even skipped lectures and spent the day working on the boat she was beginning to love more and more each time she went onboard.

##

Jed

It ended up being four weeks before Jed could get away from the mine near Port Hedland in Western Australia. He hadn't spoken to Eva since he'd got back from the States because his phone had been out of service range for most of the month, and guilt tugged at him as he flew direct to Brisbane. She'd be back at uni now, maybe. He wasn't sure when the semester began.

He frowned, realising how little attention he'd paid to the things that mattered to his wife.

Before they went home—or he went alone, if the semester had started— he was going to surprise her with a weekend in Brisbane. The more time Eva spent at her course the more uncomfortable Jed was; he knew how she hated living in Bylington.

The other alternative for his planned career path was for them to move to a remote mine in Western Australia, but at this stage he wasn't even going to consider that. She would have to give up her course and move to the remote outback; for the time being Bylington would tick all the boxes.

As soon as Jed was off the plane and in the terminal at Brisbane airport, he dialled Eva's mobile. He yawned as it rang and headed for the coffee bar at the arrivals lounge. A quick coffee, and then he'd go down to the rental car counter. As he stood in the queue, the message went to her voicemail, and disappointment rippled through him.

'Surprise! I'm in Brisbane at the airport. Picking up a rental. Where are you? Call me. Love you.' He left a voice message, cursing himself for not ringing her last night. Maybe she was back in Bylington.

By the time Jed had finished his coffee, picked up a rental and was driving into the city, his disappointment ramped up. He paired his phone to Bluetooth on the hire car, and every few minutes, he tried Eva's number, but there was no answer.

The traffic was heavy, and it took almost an hour to get through the city and across to the university. He parked the car in the almost empty residential hall car park and headed across to the building at the back where Eva lived during the semester.

The front door of the building was locked, and frustration filled Jed as he looked around. There was no-one in sight. He pushed the buzzer and eventually someone answered.

'Yo!' A deep male voice boomed through the loud music at the other end of the call.

'Hi. I'm after Eva Stephenson. Do you know if she's in?'

'Sorry mate. No-one's here. Everyone's checked out for the winter break. Uni starts up the week after next.'

'Thanks.' He walked back to the car, dejection

dogging his footsteps.

So much for a surprise. Eva must have gone home. On the way back to the airport, to return the rental and catch a flight to Dubbo, he called her mobile again, and then their land line, but there was no answer to either.

The first niggle of worry tugged at him and he dialled Zeke's number, and Samantha answered.

'Hi Sam, it's Jed. I'm on my way home. Have you talked to Eva in the last few days?'

'Hi, Jed. Zeke talked to her and their Grandpa last night. She's staying with him in Brisbane.'

'Oh, okay. Thanks. I'll keep trying her number.'

'Good luck. Zeke was roaring at her for letting her phone go flat last night too. He talked to her on their grandpa's phone.'

'Do you have his number?'

'Zeke does. I'll get him to text it to you when he comes in for lunch.'

'Thanks. See you soon We'll be home in a couple of days.'

'Bye, mate.'

Samantha was a decent girl, and she loved the farm life. Jed was disappointed that Eva didn't spend more time over there when he was away, but Eva and Zeke were usually fighting about something or other.

With a sigh, he headed back to the city; he'd book into their usual hotel while he waited to get in touch with his wife.

Chapter Twenty

Eva – eight years earlier

The radio was blaring beside her as Eva varnished the handrail around the back deck. As she leaned forward to carefully brush the last corner, a hand tapped her shoulder. With a squeal she dropped the brush and spun around.

Her eyes widened as she looked up into the smiling face of her husband.

'Jed! Oh my God! What are you doing here?'

His smile faded, but she jumped up and threw her arms around his neck.

'I thought you had another week in Port Hedland,' she said as she kissed him. 'I've been counting the weeks.'

Jed hugged her back, then pulled away to look at her. Eva reached up to wipe her face with the back of her hand. She had a sticky smudge on her cheek, and what hair wasn't tucked into a faded baseball cap was in a tangled mess. She'd been too busy getting the boat finished to do much else.

'We finished early,' he said. 'So, I thought I'd

surprise you. Where's your phone? I left a couple of messages.'

'Um.' She screwed up her nose and thought. 'In my bag below deck, I think. I've had the radio on all morning.' She stepped back and noticed her grandfather on the wharf. 'Ah, I wondered how you found me.'

'That almost sounds as though you were hiding.' Despite his smile Jed's voice held a note she hadn't heard before.

Impatience? Disappointment?

'Thanks to your brother, his wife and your grandfather, I did find you.' This time there was an edge to his voice. 'And *Eros*, your boat, I believe, Eva?'

'Oh yes. I have lots of news for you.' Warmth ran up her neck, and it wasn't from the sun. 'Grandpa. Come aboard.' She looked to Jed. 'I take it you two have met?'

'We have. Your grandfather told me how he gave you his boat. *A few months ago.*' This time the impatience in Jed's voice had gone to steel. 'Mentioning it to me must have slipped your mind.'

Grandpa raised his eyebrows and headed down to the galley. 'I'll put the kettle on.'

Jed stood beside her until Grandpa was out of

sight, and then he turned to her. 'What's going on, Eva? Should I worry?'

She shook her head. 'Worry about what? There's nothing to hide. I have a boat now. You were away for over three months, so I decided to stay here and do some work.'

'You weren't going to sail off into the sunset?'

This time irritation—with a bit of guilt in the mix—crept in. 'Of course, I wasn't. What was the point in going home to rattle around a huge and spotlessly clean house if you weren't there? Now that Grandpa has moved to Brisbane, I have some company here.'

Eva tensed as she stood there and waited for Jed's reaction. She relaxed when his arms went around her, and he held her close. She nestled into him and appreciated the tenderness in his hold.

'I'm sorry I was away so long, babe. I missed you so much,' he said.

'I missed you too,' she whispered. 'But can you see why I stayed here?'

He nodded. 'Unfortunately, I can. I'm sorry for being cross. And I'm sorry that I was away for so long. We had a lot of problems over there in the west.'

'I was going to tell you about *Eros,* and Grandpa

when I got home. It wasn't the sort of thing I wanted to tell you over the phone.'

Jed's mouth was close to her ear. 'Let's have a quick cuppa and then go back to the hotel. I've booked our usual suite for the weekend.'

Eva would have preferred to stay on *Eros*—with Jed—but she didn't think it was the time to say that. 'That sounds good, and then how about we come back here tomorrow, and I'll take you out for a sail?'

He nodded, but by his expression she wondered if he was keen.

'We don't have to. I'll just finish off this bit of varnishing while you have a cuppa with Grandpa. I have to finish it before we go.'

Her heart sank as Jed's reply set the tone for the next couple of days.

'Okay, let's see what tomorrow brings.'

Chapter Twenty-One

Evie - Pentecost Island

When Evie left Jed in the bar, she'd headed back to the house. Sienna and Eliza, Tam, Nell and Pippa were sitting quietly on the veranda, waiting for her.

Evie placed the tray with their dinner dishes carefully on the table, put her hands over her eyes and began to cry. Pippa jumped up and her arms went around Evie.

'Was it so bad, Evie?' she asked quietly.

Evie lifted her head and saw the tears in the eyes of each one of her friends as they watched her cry in Pippa's arms. She stepped back and wiped her eyes with the back of her hand. Sienna grabbed the box of tissues on the table.

Eva took one and nodded her thanks and then wiped her face. 'I have to go to Brisbane. Jed came to tell me.' Her voice broke. 'My brother, Zeke, is dying, and if I'm a match with my bone marrow I might be able to save his life.'

Tam poured a glass of wine and patted the seat beside her. 'Come and sit down and tell us how we can help.'

Evie nodded. 'But only one drink. I have a lot of work to do tonight.'

The support of her friends as they surrounded her with love was one of the most special moments of her life. 'Thank you,' she said as she lifted her glass and the tears began to run down her cheeks again.

Oh, Zeke.

##

'A couple of metres of garden soil, too, please, Pippa. If I think of anything else, I'll text you from Brisbane.' Evie handed over the list that she'd typed up on Nell's computer, with the quantities she required, and the preferred suppliers. She'd worked until midnight, drawing up plans, work schedules and lists of equipment and plants.

Jed had managed to book two seats on the early flight out of Hamilton Island tomorrow and Evie was finalising the landscape supplies order for Pippa to place while she was away.

'The only other thing I need to know is if you've decided on a colour scheme for the wedding.'

Tamsin and Nell had come back to the office to keep them company while Evie worked, and both chimed in together. 'Not pink!'

Sienna was sitting in the living room and she echoed their words.

Pippa pulled a face at them. 'That's correct. Not pink.' She reached out and took Evie's hand. 'If you can't come back in time to do the work, it's not a problem. Your brother and your family are more important than a garden.'

'And your wedding is important too,' Evie shook her head emphatically. 'I'll be back to have the grounds perfect. I'll hire someone to do the mowing while I'm away, and I'll keep them on until the wedding. I'll let you know when I'll be back as soon as I know what's happening.' She frowned and looked at Pippa. 'Take the cost out of my wages.'

'Don't be silly. And *I'll* organise someone to mow. You just focus on what you have to do. What time's your flight? The eight a.m.?'

'Yes.'

'Rafe will take you over. That way you won't have to pay for a berth for your boat at the marina.'

'Thank you. I'm going to go to bed now.' Evie frowned at Pippa. 'Pippa, don't walk up to the house by yourself. Call Rafe and get him to come down and walk you home.'

'He's waiting for me to call,' she replied.

'On your way back, can you stop at Jed's hut and let him know to meet us at the wharf? What do you think? About six?'

'Six will give you enough time to get there and check in. And yes, we'll stop at the hut on the way back.' Pippa screwed up her nose. 'We're going to have to stop calling them "the huts" and use the names we decided on. It sounds a bit second rate to call them the huts, don't you think?'

'It does a bit. Serenity, Peace, and Tranquillity have much more appeal.' Evie stood and stretched. 'Night all. I'll see you when I get back.'

Nell came over and hugged her. 'We'll be thinking of you, Evie,' she said. 'If you ever need to talk, don't hesitate to call, no matter what time of day or night.'

Tam squeezed Evie's hand as she walked past. 'You take care, girlfriend.'

Evie bit her lip as moisture pricked behind her eyes, but she fought it. There'd been more than enough tears tonight. 'Thank you. I appreciate every word and thought. It's going to be tough, and I'll be pleased when

I'm back here with you all.'

Sienna stood and held her arms open as Evie walked through the living room. 'Go safely, Evie. Eliza said to give you her best too.'

'I'll see you soon.' Evie cleared her throat. 'Oh, have you picked a name for the spa yet? I've had some ideas for an all-white garden around the building.'

'Oh, yes. Sounds great. And yes, I have, and the boss has approved it'—Sienna flicked a grin at Pippa who was standing in the doorway— 'our spa is going to be called "*Hebe*", and the tag line will have something about goddess of youth and beauty in it.'

'I love it. I'll look at some plant catalogues so the white flowering shrubs can be ready to put in as soon as it's up.'

Evie walked down the hall to her room. Her hands were trembling as she opened the door. Having friends how cared was a new experience for her.

It sounded a bit twee, but she felt protected by the love that the girls surrounded her with. Coming to work on Pentecost Island had been one of the best life choices she'd ever made. It was a unique place made even more special by the group of women who had accepted her as their friend. Evie closed the door behind her and crossed to the window.

She could see Jed's hut from here, and she stood looking at it for a long time before she pulled out her bag and packed a few clothes to take to Brisbane tomorrow. Luckily, she kept most of her stuff in the house now. If she'd had to go over to the boat tonight, she would have been tempted to sail far, far away.

Jed frightened her. Not the man himself, but the feelings that she still held for him. Evie had never stopped loving him, and she knew the next few days were going to be very hard in more ways than one.

As hard as the day she had left her husband and sailed away on *Eros*.

Chapter Twenty-Two

Eva - eight years earlier

'You decided to come back after all, did you, Evangelina?' Zeke's tone was resentful as it always seemed to be lately. 'I thought you liked the big smoke better than home.'

Jed and Eva were standing at the gate at the front yard of the farm. No one had been home when they knocked on the door and then they'd heard Zeke's motorbike coming up from the back paddock and had waited. They'd only arrived home from Brisbane three hours before and had taken the phone call that would change her life. Grandpa had died, not long after Jed and Eva had said goodbye to him and left Brisbane to drive to Bylington.

'Back off, mate.' Jed stepped beside Eva and put his arm around her.

Zeke's eyes widened but he shut up.

'We've got some bad news.' Eva kept her voice calm. 'Grandpa passed away this morning. He was in Brisbane and we saw him before we left.'

'At least you got to see him,' Zeke said

resentfully. 'Not that he would have cared about not seeing me before he carked it. The old codger was never interested in me.'

Evie couldn't hold back. 'Oh, for God's sake, Zeke. Can you ever think of anyone apart from yourself?'

Her brother looked at her, his eyes narrowed and then he shrugged. 'Okay. I'm sorry he died, but I haven't seen him for years.'

'You need to know, he gave me his boat when he came back to Brisbane, and I know he looked after you in his will. He told me that a few weeks ago when he was worried about you being jealous of me having the boat.'

'Jesus, what would I do with an old tub? You're welcome to it.' He had the grace to look apologetic. 'Look, I'm sorry for snapping. I haven't had a good day. I lost my best bull this morning.'

Eve nodded but said nothing. She and Jed hadn't had a good day either. The trip home from Brisbane had been travelled mostly in silence. They hadn't argued, but she knew Jed wasn't happy with her.

The problem was she didn't care, and then when the call came about Grandpa, it was as though her whole heart was encased in ice. She didn't care about anything, and after only seven hours of leaving the boat behind, she yearned to be back on the water.

Her mood had worsened as they got closer to Bylington. The countryside looked harsh; the grass that had held a vestige of green when she'd left at the end of summer was now dry and brown. The whole landscape was drab and depressing; drought had taken hold of the central west and the frosts of winter had finished it off. A tiny burst of sympathy melted the hardness around her heart; no wonder Zeke was doing it tough.

'Do you want to come in for a cuppa? Sam'll be home soon.'

'No, thanks. We've just got home, and I'm tired.'

'Okay. Well, let me know when the funeral is. I'll try and get there, but I can't promise.'

Eva nodded and headed back to Jed's car, and left the two men talking. She knew they were talking about her, because Zeke kept looking over at the car. But she didn't care. She didn't care about anything. All she wanted to do was turn around and leave.

##

To his credit, Jed tried.

He tried so hard that Eva loved him even more.

And that made it harder for her. She fought hard to be happy, but it was impossible. She knew now, no matter how much she loved Jed, their marriage wasn't going to work. She felt so confined back in Bylington, and back in their house, it was hard to breathe.

The first night after they came home, she and Jed lay side by side in their bed, not touching. Eva knew he was awake beside her, and she knew he was hurting, but she had nothing to give.

They each wanted different things. Jed was happy in the house, and happy in Bylington, and focused on his career. Eva needed to be on the coast near the water. She had no one to talk to, and she lay there thinking of her mother and how she'd stayed with Reg, even though Mum had realised that she had made a mistake marrying him.

Her situation with Jed was different; she couldn't compare him to her stepfather. Jed Stephenson was a good man, and Eva knew he loved her and would probably leave his career for her, if she'd asked.

But she knew that wasn't fair.

As she lay there in their king-size bed, hot tears seeped from the corners of her eyes and ran down onto the pillow. She lay there and let them come, until her nose was so clogged, she had to get up and go to the bathroom for a tissue.

When she came back, Jed's back was turned to her, and Eva lay there thinking of all she had lost.

She cried for her mother, and her Grandpa, and for a brother who didn't care about his family.

But most of all, she cried for what she was about to do to the man she loved.

Chapter Twenty-Three

Jed

Jed was outside looking at the water when Pippa had walked past with Rafe after midnight and told him to be at the wharf at six a.m.

He was packed at dawn and walked over at five-thirty and sat on the rock at the base of the steps that led up to the house on the hill.

He hadn't had much sleep since he'd been on the island. Last night as he'd sat outside watching the water, his thoughts filled with Eva—Evie—he corrected himself again. She was even more beautiful now than she had been ten years ago when he had fallen in love with her. He'd known then she was a damaged soul, but their first months together had been happy, and she'd settled into his house. Foolishly, he thought they could overcome her demons together.

They could both take blame for the disintegration of their relationship. If he'd not been so focused on his damn career and been away so much, and if Evie hadn't chosen to begin that university course—she'd only attended for two semesters—maybe they could have worked harder at making their marriage work.

He thought about his life now, and knew if he'd made that decision back then, they would have had a chance.

The Evie that he'd seen over the last two days— after their initial meeting anyway— had poise and confidence and had obviously settled into a life that made her happy. He was grateful that she had a good job, on a beautiful island, and was obviously supported by a group of strong women friends. He'd seen how they protected her.

'Good morning.'

Jed jumped as the subject of his thoughts stepped up onto the wharf. He'd been so engrossed in the past he hadn't heard her coming. 'Good morning.'

'You're early too,' she said.

'Yes. I woke before dawn. There was a strange bird crying outside my hut.'

'A curlew,' she replied. 'They do have an interesting call.'

Silence descended and he hunted around for something to fill it.

Before he could speak, Evie did. 'Do you like

our island?'

'Very much. I can see why you're happy working here. I heard that you've done all the landscaping.'

'Yes, it's a great job. It's been a satisfying few months.'

'You've travelled a bit over the past couple of years, haven't you?'

'Been keeping tabs on me, Jed?'

'No, not keeping tabs, I just wanted to know that you were okay. You've never touched any of the money I put in your account, have you?'

'No, because I told you it was unnecessary.' She held his gaze steadily. 'We should have divorced and then you wouldn't have had to worry.'

'Do you think that would have made a difference to me wanting to know you were alright?' He lifted one hand and ran it through his hair in frustration. 'It was all right for you, doing what you loved and what you wanted, and not reporting to anyone. Not letting anyone know where you were. Christ, Evie, every time I read about an abandoned yacht, or a pirate attack in Indonesia, or a fire in a marina, I worried if it was you.'

She shrugged. 'I can look after myself.'

The silence was heavy this time, and he let out a relieved breath when Pippa and her partner, Rafe, came down the steps.

'Morning,' Rafe said as Pippa walked over to Evie. 'All ready to go?'

'I'm coming too,' Pippa said. 'To do some shopping and meet with the builders. By the time we see you off, and my lovely man takes me out for breakfast, the shops will be open.'

'Yes, we're ready,' Jed replied. 'Thanks for taking us over. Please add it to my bill. I've left my credit card details at the office.'

Pippa waved her hand. 'Don't be silly. You paid for a week, and you've only been here two nights. Please consider those five nights as credit and come back and stay with us when this is all over.'

Evie looked over and Jed caught the expression on her face as she nodded. To his surprise, she didn't look too unhappy about that prospect.

He nodded too. 'That would be good, thank you.'

'I suppose you've got holidays and long service leave up your sleeve now.' Evie glanced at Pippa. 'Jed rarely takes time off.'

Irritation niggled at Jed. 'You might be surprised these days, Evie. Being my own boss, I can take time off whenever I want. I'll definitely come back here. After.'

They were all quiet. The "after" was an unknown until they discovered if Evie could be a donor for her brother.

Rafe started the motor and the other three sat on the leather lounge at the back of his boat.

'What do you mean your own boss?' Evie asked.

'I had a career change.'

Her eyes widened. 'Aren't you still with the mines though?'

'No. I left the mining industry when I left Bylington eighteen months after you did. I've been back over the past couple of years to help out on the farm when Zeke was having his treatment.'

Evie looked away. 'I didn't know that.'

It was the most interest she'd shown in him since Jed had arrived on the island.

'What sort of job do you do? Mine consulting?' she asked softly as she looked at him

'No.' He held her eyes, willing her not to look away again. 'I followed my dream. Just like you followed yours, Evie.'

Chapter Twenty-Four

Evie – Brisbane

The flight from Hamilton Island to Brisbane was quick, and as the plane began its descent into Brisbane airport, Evie's stomach knotted. The last time she had seen her brother was the day she had left Jed, and Bylington, eight years ago. She'd made the mistake of going over to the farm to tell Zeke what she was doing. She'd thought that they had enough of a relationship for him to understand.

What she needed.

And how lost she was.

His reaction had been absolutely over the top. Zeke's nostrils had flared as he'd yelled at her. Eva had taken a step back, as he'd flexed his fingers as though he was going to punch her.

Maybe he'd learned more from their stepfather than she'd realised. He turned away from her and punched the side of the house so hard she'd been surprised he didn't break his hand.

When he turned back, a vein pulsed in Zeke's forehead. 'If you leave Jed, and you leave this town, you will be lost to me, Evangelina.' His eyes had been cold and hard, and his voice low and controlled. 'Don't even bother contacting me. Ever,' he spat.

Without a word, she turned and walked to her car. The car that her husband had bought for her when she told him she was leaving.

The thud of the aircraft's wheels coming down from the undercarriage jerked her from her thoughts.

It was a rough landing and when Evie gasped, Jed put his hand out and took hers.

'You're very nervous, aren't you?'

'About meeting Zeke, yes.' She let Jed hold her hand and tried to ignore the lightness that filled her. 'Am I that obvious?'

Jed's voice was soft as the "Welcome to Brisbane" message came over the system. 'We might have only been together for a very short part of our lives, but I still know what makes you tick. I'll bet your stomach is churning and you're going over all of Zeke's possible reactions.'

'I am. Does he have to agree to me being a donor if I match? What if he says no?'

'I don't know. That's one of the questions you'll have to ask. But Evie, stop worrying. Zeke has mellowed. He's a good husband, and a wonderful father to his two little boys. If there is any chance of him finding a treatment that works, he won't knock it back.'

Evie bit her lip and her voice shook. 'What if he won't speak to me?'

'He will. He loves you, swee—Evie. When I caught up with you each time I managed to find you, Zeke always wanted to know where you were and what you were doing.' His eyes crinkled in a grin. 'When I knew where you were anyway. I never told you about the time that I saw *Eros*. Mum and Dad's house isn't far from the northern headland. I was sitting out having a beer one afternoon and I saw you sail across Moreton Bay. At first I wasn't sure if it was your boat because of the hot pink sail, but even from half a kilometre, when you came out on the deck, I recognised you.'

'The pink sail was part of a breast cancer race I supported a few years back.' She clasped his hand tightly. 'You should have come and said hello when I came in.'

His laugh held no mirth. 'Really?'

'Okay, probably not.' She shrugged and looked down. 'As hard as it might be to accept, I've mellowed too, Jed. I never had any hard feelings towards you. I carried a lot of guilt because I knew I should never have married you. That's why I got upset the few times I saw you. I stuffed up your life for a while.'

His response was instant. 'I disagree. I wouldn't trade that one year, nine months and four days for anything,' he said softly.

Before she could reply the seatbelt light flicked off, and Jed let go of her hand as they gathered their hand luggage and prepared to disembark. There was a crowd at the baggage carousels, and his hand was firm against her back as he guided her to the carousel at the far end.

Soon they had collected their bags and were heading to the multistorey car park where Jed explained he'd left his vehicle when he'd flown north in search of her.

Evie was expecting a luxury estate car like he'd always driven, so she was surprised when he gestured towards his vehicle. The angriest words they'd exchanged when she'd left and Jed had insisted on buying her a car, had been because he's wanted to buy her an Audi, and she'd insisted on a cheap and small common sedan.

So, when he stopped behind a battered Toyota

four wheel drive, her mouth opened. She shut it quickly without commenting but did notice the grin on Jed's face. Her nose wrinkled when he opened the passenger door for her, and a strong sharp smell wafted out.

'That's marine varnish,' she commented curiously.

'No, it's decking oil.' He didn't elaborate further.

Evie stretched her legs out and ignored the pile of paint-stained rags on the floor of the passenger side. She turned slightly and looked in the back of the long vehicle. Pots of paint and varnish, and odd-sized pieces of timber filled the rest of the vehicle.

'This is your vehicle?'

He nodded as he started the engine, put it into gear and backed it out of the small space. 'It is.'

It was like playing twenty questions. 'So, this is your *work* vehicle?' she asked as he negotiated the ramp down towards the boom gate at the exit.

Jed dug into his pocket and flipped open his wallet, pulled out a credit card and waved it over the sensor, and soon they were on the main road into the city.

'This is my work vehicle, and my recreational

vehicle. My *only* vehicle. It was Dad's and I figured that she had a few years left in her yet.'

'Oh.'

The grin he shot her way was wide. He was still a good-looking man and a warm shiver ran down Evie's spine when Jed glanced at her again. 'I like surprising you.'

'Well, I'm surprised.' It was good to be having a light-hearted conversation and it was taking Evie's mind off their destination. 'You said you followed your dream. I was immature and selfish when we were married. Why didn't I ever know what your dream was?'

'We were young, Evie. And'—heat crept up her neck as he slid another sideways glance at her— 'we were in love and we were busy.'

'Yes, but you knew me so well. You knew what my problems were, and you knew what I loved doing, and what my dreams were. Did we ever talk about you? What you wanted to do? What your dreams were?'

'I was happy the way we were. I was happy when you were happy. That's why I didn't fight when you wanted to leave. I wanted you to be happy, and I knew I wasn't enough for you. It hurt, but I knew I had to let you go.'

All of a sudden, their conversation was intense.

'I'm sorry. I didn't mean for us to get so heavy, so quickly,' he said.

'No, it was me. I feel so bad. What was your dream, Jed?'

As she waited, she noticed colour stain his cheeks.

'You'll probably think it's silly. I mean, I did all that study. An honours degree in engineering, and all those trips to the western mines and overseas, and then I gave it all away.'

'For?' She raised her eyebrows.

'To follow my dream and learn what happiness is.' His hands were tight on the steering wheel, and Evie's gaze lingered on his strong forearms.

'And did it work?' she asked softly.

'Almost. I'm getting there. I'll be honest. Even though it's been eight years, I still miss you every day, Evie.' His knuckles were white, and she realised that although he was keeping his tone light, Jed was tense. 'Tell me if I'm out of line. Do you ever think about me?'

'Often.' She looked down at her hands in her lap. 'But I always imagined you in that house and your job at Bylington. It's a bit of a shock to know that you're in Brisbane and that you are doing . . . um . . . deck painting?'

Jed's laugh surrounded them, and Evie couldn't help but smile with him. 'What? You're not a deck painter.'

'No.' He shook his head. 'I'm a furniture craftsman, and I've done quite well, even if I do say so myself.'

'Wow. You've really surprised me. I had no idea. How does it work?

'I take orders. I build what the client requests, and each set is a one-off.'

Evie tapped her lip with one finger as she thought. 'How long would it take you—' she shook her head. 'No, it doesn't matter. You're probably busy.'

'How long would it take me to what?'

'Well, we were all—not Pippa—trying to think of a unique wedding present for her and Rafe. I was going to do a little nook in their garden with some rare tropical shrubs, and we were going to look for a small table and two chairs. Just for them.'

'I'd be honoured. They seem like a great couple.'

Evie nodded. 'They have been very good to me.'

'Don't discredit yourself. I was talking to Nell one day and she told me that you've done all that landscaping.' He chuckled. 'And believe me. I have walked a lot of that island looking for you. You've done some beautiful work.'

'Thank you. I'd like to see some of yours too.'

'I've got a shed over at Manly. You're quite welcome to stay at my house. I hope you will.'

Evie's throat closed as Jed turned into a private hospital and she realised they had arrived.

'Oh, shit,' she said.

Chapter Twenty-Five

Pippa

When Rafe and I were over on Hamilton Island after seeing Evie and Jed off at the airport, we took the opportunity of meeting with the Riccardos, and the news was great.

Well, great for us, but not so great for their job that had been cancelled. But what it meant for Ma Carmichael's was that as soon as the supplies were delivered—and they were on order and ready to be sent from the mainland—the Riccardo Brothers could start work.

Danny Riccardo shook my hand as we left the office. 'I guarantee with my crew, we can have your work completed in four weeks. Tops.'

'All of it? The restaurant, the huts and the spa?'

'Yes, I've got a great team, and they work fast, but the quality is not compromised. We'll pour the concrete in three days.'

I swallowed and put my arm through Rafe's as we walked back towards the restaurant strip. 'Are we being silly? Should we wait until after the wedding?'

'Sweetheart,' he said in that gorgeous plummy accent that I loved so much. 'As much as I am delighted about, and looking forward to our wedding, in reality it is only one day of island life. If we get rain, or any other holdups, it's not going to impact on the ceremony. If indeed the work is finished, can you imagine Tamsin, when she may have the possibility of catering in a commercial kitchen, and having the reception in a real building?'

'As usual, you are *indeed* right,' I said teasing him.

Rafe put his arm around me and held me close. 'You'll pay for that later, wench,' he joked.

'Take me to breakfast, and then take me home.' I reached up and kissed him as we walked along.

Life had been hectic at Ma Carmichael's over the past few months, not to mention a bit on the dramatic side. Our itinerant population had grown since the girls had met their partners. Gabe and Nat were due to come over this weekend, and we'd all be there except for Evie.

Rafe held my chair out after we'd chosen a popular marina café with a view. He was always the gentleman and sometimes I had to pinch myself to believe this man loved me. As we'd walked along the street a lot of female heads had turned, and I puffed up with pride.

'What are you smiling about?' he asked as he sat down opposite me and poured a glass of water from the carafe on the table.

'Just happy,' I said as I looked around. 'Everything is going so well. Touch wood.' I tapped my knuckles on the table. 'I'm just hoping that we get good news from Evie after she sees the doctor. I do hope she can help her brother.'

'What did you think of Jed?' Rafe asked.

'I liked him. I'd heard a lot about him from Evie when we were at uni, and she always spoke very highly of him.'

'So, they've known each other for a while? I thought they might have been more than friends. I saw the way he was looking at Evie.'

'Oh, I forgot you didn't know.' I put my hand over my mouth.

'Know what?'

'They're married.'

'Married? So, what's Evie doing working for us on the island?'

'They've been separated for a long time, but

never divorced. I was pleased to hear Jed say he would come back. I'm hoping our island might work its magic spell.'

'And what spell would that be, you hopeless romantic?' Rafe picked my hand up and brushed his lips over my open palm, and my legs went to jelly.

'A romantic spell. Anyone can see that they're meant to be together.'

'Leave them be. I'm sure if it's meant to be, they'll work it out. You've got too much building work to supervise to find any time to matchmake.'

'Oh damn, I just remembered. I've got another appointment too, while we're here. What time is it?'

'Nine thirty.'

'Phew, we've got time to eat before I meet Cherry at ten.'

'Cherry? Honestly, Phillipa, I can't keep up with you. You're going to wear me out.'

'And I'll love every minute of it,' I said cheekily. 'It's not too late to change your mind about the wedding.'

'No chance, love. Now who's Cherry?'

'Cherry Chilcott. She's coming to work for us in the new restaurant.'

Rafe smiled at me indulgently and gestured for the waitress. 'You just tell me what I have to do, and I'll accommodate you.'

I leaned over and whispered in his ear, and I couldn't help giggle when he blushed.

'Behave, Miss Carmichael!'

Chapter Twenty- Six

Evie – Brisbane

Evie had hated hospitals since she was fourteen and her mother had gone into one and had never come home. As she walked across the bland grey carpet beside Jed, their footsteps were soundless; they were surrounded only by the regular hospital noises and antiseptic smells. Hushed voices, beeping machines and the sound of a tea trolley being pushed up the adjacent corridor broke the silence.

Evie fought the nausea that was rising in her stomach, and silver lights began to prick at the side of her vision the further they walked down the hall. An awful cold feeling filled her chest, and she thought she was going to vomit. She stopped walking, took a deep breath before crossing her arms over her stomach.

Before she knew it, Jed had taken her across to a chair in a small waiting room and pushed her head gently down between her knees. Her hands were trembling, but she began to feel better straight away as the blood began to circulate through her body.

'Are you okay, sweetheart?' His voice was close

to her ear, and soothing; his arm was tight around her shoulders as she began to sit up.

'Yes, that awful faint feeling has passed. It's only stress. Once I see Zeke, I'll be fine.' She sat up straighter. 'Could you get me some water, please.'

Jed jumped up and was soon back with a bottle of cold water.

Evie drank deeply, and she could feel the warmth come back into her body. 'Okay. I'm fine now. Let's do this. Is it far?'

Jed shook his head. 'Last week Zeke was in Ward Eight, about five down from here.' He held his hand out, and it felt natural for Evie to put her hand in his. He held it tightly and the last eight years seemed to dissolve in some sort of time slip.

When they reached the room, Jed gestured for her to stay at the door, and he leaned around and checked it was still where Zeke was.

He turned to her with a nod. 'He's awake.'

Jed stepped back and let Evie walk in first.

She forced a smile onto her face and approached the bed in the private room. Zeke was lying on his side, hooked up to a a drip as he stared through the large window to a small, but colourful garden.

'Hello, big brother.' Evie stopped beside the bed, and Zeke turned his head slowly to look at her. She kept the smile on her face until Zeke lifted his right hand and reached out to her. A tear rolled down his face as he tried to speak.

His voice was husky when he finally got his breath. 'Evangelina. I knew you were coming today.'

'Did Jed tell you I was on the way?' she asked shakily. Zeke's face was puffed, and his head was almost bald, only a few tufts of hair showing near his forehead.

'No. I dreamed about you. I dreamed you came, and I told you I was sorry. I had to tell you in case—'

'No. What's happened in the past stays in the past. I love you, Zeke.' Evie tried to smile but it turned into a sob.

Between tests and meetings, Evie spent each afternoon with her brother, and then went home to Jed's house in the early evening each day. When they'd arrived on the first night after leaving the hospital, he'd shown her to a large guest room with its own ensuite and a small kitchenette in the corner, on the lower level adjacent to the garage.

'That way you can be independent if you want. There's tea and coffee and bread in the cupboard, and fresh milk, butter and jam in the fridge. I hoped you might stay here so I bought ginger marmalade,' Jed said. 'If you need anything just call. My room is upstairs.'

She guessed he was telling her that she was not too close to him.

After a few days, Evie felt at home and their days fell into a routine. Some mornings she went upstairs and sat on the veranda with Jed and they had coffee together looking over the Bay before they went to the hospital.

Evie appreciated that Jed always kept the conversation very general. He asked her about the places she'd been, and the work she'd done in Vanuatu.

'Where to after Pentecost Island?' he asked one morning as he stood to take her empty coffee mug back to the kitchen.

'I'm pretty settled there. I'll probably stay a while longer yet.' She looked up at him as he nodded. 'What about you. Will you stay here?'

He took a while to answer. 'I guess I will. I'm well set up here. My workshop is close by, and I've got a storage shed behind it.'

Evie couldn't help herself. 'So that's your work. What about your social life? Do you go out much?' She swallowed. 'Are you seeing anyone?

His smile faded. 'I'm still married. Would it matter to you if I was seeing someone? What about you? Are you seeing anyone?' Jed turned and went back to the kitchen before she could answer.

Well, that went well, she thought. But it made her think about things that she'd blocked for a long time. Maybe it was time to insist on a divorce so they could both move on. Jed was young enough to marry again and have a family.

Evie was quite happy with what she was doing.

I am, she tried to convince herself.

When Jed came back out jiggling the car keys, the subject wasn't raised again. 'Ready?'

She'd bring it up one night when he was more approachable.

##

Evie willed the days to go faster so that the transplant could take place; she could see Zeke getting weaker as each day passed. She felt like she was in a holding pattern and thoughts of the urgency of her work at Pentecost Island receded. Zeke was her priority.

Jed was amazing. He drove her to the clinics for the various tests; he looked after her two nephews while Sam spent time with Zeke, and he cooked Evie a meal each night. His house was a high set old Queenslander, and he'd been self-conscious as he'd showed her some of the furniture he'd made for the house.

'I thought you said you made outdoor furniture,' she said as she looked at the beautiful pieces in his living room.

'Yes, outdoor furniture is my business, these are just for me. They're not good enough to sell.'

Evie ran her hand over the coffee table. It was smooth and so highly glossed she could almost see her reflection in it. 'You're doing yourself a disservice. You're very talented, Jed.'

'It pays the bills,' he said.

'Don't you have any work you have to do? You've been driving me around all week.'

'No, I've given myself time off while you're here and until Zeke has the transplant.' He looked over at her, and a wave of love washed over Evie.

She walked over and put her hand on his shoulder. 'You're a good man, Jed.'

He lifted his hand and put it on hers; they stood

there together, and he held her eyes until Evie turned away.

'I'll go and check on dinner,' he said quietly.

Something had shifted between them, and Evie found it difficult to get to sleep that night. Spending so much time with Jed in his home was strange. Strange, in that it felt natural. The silence between them was easy now, and her respect for Jed grew daily as she watched him interact with the two small boys, and Sam.

Sometimes, she had to pull herself up as she went to do things that she would have done naturally when they were living together. A gentle touch, a look, a hug—the actions all tempted her, and she had to fight not to give in.

When she climbed into bed at night, she longed to feel Jed's arms around her.

Nothing had changed, she told herself. It was the fear of losing Zeke plus the strange situation of living with her ex-husband–not ex, she told herself— it was the situation that was making her feel needy, not any resurgence of a relationship.

Chapter Twenty-Seven

Evie

The ten days before the procedure were hectic. Evie met with the doctor, had the blood test, and to her delight, she was a perfect match bone marrow match for Zeke. She had a long session with the donor information officer where she learned about the process and the risks, to ensure she was making an informed decision. Once she signed the consent forms, she had a full medical and the procedure was set for the middle of the second week after she'd arrived.

Despite the upcoming medical procedure, Evie relaxed more each day. She and Zeke had talked and talked, and he'd shared his hopes—and fears—with her.

On the day before the procedure, the two of them were alone in the private room. As Jed had told her, Zeke had grown into a mature and level-headed man, nothing like the hot-headed, angry brother she'd grown up with.

'We did it tough, didn't we, sis? Losing Dad, and then Mum and then living with that cranky bugger for five years. No wonder we ended up so screwed up.'

'Hey, speak for yourself,' Evie said, nudging him 'I'm not screwed up.'

'Maybe not now, but you were back then. You broke Jed's heart and left the pieces for Sam and me to pick up.'

'Jed was happy to let me go, Zeke. I don't want to talk about it. It's all in the past now.'

'It's not, you know. And we are going to talk about it, Eva.' He looked at her with a devious smile 'This could be my last chance to say what I want to.'

'Stop it, don't say that,' she yelled and a nurse who was walking past paused at the door.

Zeke waved her away. 'It's okay, Geraldine. My sister and I are just having a discussion. One we need to have.'

The nurse nodded and kept walking.

Evie's cheeks burned with embarrassment and she stood. 'It's time I was going. Jed's probably waiting in the car park.'

'Sit down, Evangelina.'

Evie bit her lip and did as her brother asked.

'You might have been swanning around the islands, burying your head in the sand, but you need to hear a few things,' he said quietly. 'You need to know that even though I roared at you the day you left it was because I understood exactly what you were doing and why you felt that way. I let you down. You were only fourteen when Mum died. I saw how you shut yourself away. You had no friends, and Reg worked you so bloody hard in the house.'

'It's okay, I survived.' Evie lifted her chin and looked at her brother. 'You don't need to take the blame for anything.'

'I do,' he said. 'I did let you down. I was trying to prove I was a big man. I drank too much, and I bossed you around. The more I hurt you, it sort of made me hurt less. I can understand it now, but I was an absolute bastard to you. No wonder you ran for the first man who showed any kindness to you.'

Evie shook her head. 'It wasn't just that. It was more than kindness or escaping from the farm. I fell in love with Jed, Zeke. It had nothing to do with running to him.' She put her head down. 'And I know he loved me.'

'He still loves you, Eva.'

'I don't think so.' She lifted her head and held her brother's eyes. His pallor and his puffed face broke her heart. 'He's just a very kind and good man.'

'He's been a very good mate to me over the years.'

'I'm pleased to hear that.'

'So, what are you going to do about it?' Zeke asked.

'There's nothing to be done. We both have lives of our own now. Jed's happy. We can be friends.'

'Married friends?' Zeke's eyes were wide, and she was sure if he still had eyebrows they would have been raised. He leaned forward and started to cough and Evie reached for his water.

'You've talked too much. I hear what you're saying, and I'll take it on board. Okay?'

'Alright, I'll let it go now, but I want you to make me one promise. Two actually.'

Evie looked at him and fought the tears that ached behind her eyes as she looked at the man who was a pale shadow of the vital brother she'd left on the farm that awful day eight years ago. 'What?'

'If I don't make it through the transplant, or afterwards, I want you to look out for Sam and the boys.'

Evie's throat thickened and she nodded. 'Of course I will. That goes without saying.'

'I also want you to promise that you'll give Jed another chance. He loves you, Evie, he always has.'

She stared at her brother and nodded slowly.

Chapter Twenty-Eight

Evie

Zeke had been in isolation for three days and had undergone another round of chemotherapy. Samantha and the boys came over to Jed's for dinner the night before the procedure. Seeing the boys rolling around the floor with Jed made Sam and Evie laugh. After dinner, and stories for the boys, Jed drove them back to the cottage in the hospital grounds, and Evie had opted for an early night.

Sam had hugged her tightly as Jed was strapping the boys in the car. 'Thank you, Evie. We'll never be able to thank you enough for what you're doing.'

'There's no thanks required, Sam,' she said simply. 'Zeke is my brother.'

Evie woke early the next morning; she had to be at the hospital by eight. Even though it was to be a day procedure, she was aware she might have to stay overnight, so she packed a small bag and put it on the table outside the guest suite before she went upstairs in search of Jed. The front door was open, and she walked in quietly. Jed was standing in the kitchen, looking through the window.

'Good morning,' she said. 'I'm packed and ready to go.'

Jed turned slowly, and Evie's eyes widened. His face was pale, but there were two red spots high on his cheeks, and his eyes were shadowed.

'Are you sick?' she said, hurrying over. She went to put her hand on his forehead to feel if he was hot, but Jed caught it as she raised it.

'I'm fine. I just didn't sleep.'

She stared at him; he couldn't look any more different to the happy man who'd rolled around the floor with two boys on his back last night. Evie realised how much of a front Jed had been putting up to stay strong for everyone.

Before she let herself think, she slid her arms around his waist and put her head on his shoulder. Jed's hand came up and gently cupped the back of her neck, holding her close. She wouldn't let herself think about how right it felt. The familiar shoulder, the same masculine smell. She closed her eyes and took strength from him.

'It's going to be alright, Jed. We have to be positive.'

His voice was tight. 'I've been worrying about you all night. Thinking about all the things that could go wrong.'

'Nothing's going to go wrong. While I'm in theatre, go and have a coffee or go for a walk, don't sit around waiting, because the time will drag. I'll be out before you know it, and we'll be back here, and you'll be cooking my dinner.'

His arms tightened around her. 'I can't let you go in there without telling you, Evie.'

'Telling me?' She pulled back and looked up at him.

'I've never stopped loving you. I need you to know that.'

Before she could reply, Jed's arms dropped, and he moved away. 'I'll meet you at the car.'

Chapter Twenty-Nine

Evie

As it turned out, Evie's procedure was delayed until the afternoon, and she was late coming out of recovery after the anaesthetic, so she spent the night in the hospital.

Jed was waiting in the foyer when she was discharged the following morning. As soon as she saw him, Evie sensed the change in him. He took her bag and moved away from her.

'How are you feeling? The nurse said it went well when I called last night.' His tone was distant and almost disinterested. It was hard to believe this was the same man who'd held her close twenty-four hours ago and told her he loved her.

'A little bit sore in my back, but all good. I can't work for a week, so I'll stay down here for a few days after Zeke has the bone marrow transplant.'

He nodded and gestured to the door. 'Shall we go?'

He didn't speak again until they were in the car

and had turned onto the motorway towards the Bay. 'Pippa called last night, and I told her it went well. She said to tell you not to hurry back. Everything was under control.'

'Good. I'll give her a ring later.'

Jed glanced across at her. 'You look tired. Do you want to go straight to my place, or have a coffee somewhere?'

'A coffee would be good if you have time.'

He drove past his house and parked outside the coffee shop at the marina. It brought memories flooding back for Evie; she'd spent a lot of time in that coffee shop when Grandpa had given her his boat.

Jed walked around and opened her door and stood there as she climbed out of the car. He moved away again as they walked across the car park.

They ordered and took their coffees outside.

'The years have passed quickly, haven't they?'

Jed nodded and gestured to a vacant table that overlooked the water. It was almost impossible to engage him in a conversation. His eyes were hooded when he did look at her, and his answers were usually a yes or a no, until she asked him if he'd given any thought to making the wedding present for Rafe and

Pippa.

Finally, there was some life in his expression. 'Of course. What exactly did you have in mind?'

'Pippa and Rafe have an area at the back of their house that faces west. It's only a small space but I know they sit out there a lot.' She wrinkled her nose as she looked at him, and this time he didn't look away. 'I was sort of imagining something a bit intricate. A piece that celebrates their wedding day. You know, maybe their initials or something? Or is that a bit naff?'

He nodded slowly. 'I'm sure I could come up with something. Light or dark timber?

'Dark.'

'Okay, leave it with me.' He pushed his cup away and stood. 'You look tired. Why don't we go home, and you can have a sleep?'

Evie winced as she stood. Her back was throbbing; there'd be no manual work at the resort or putting up sails for a while. Jed took her arm as they walked back to the car, supporting her and a measure of peace filtered through her. Not as intimate as holding her hand, but she appreciated the warmth of his hand against her skin.

Chapter Thirty

Pippa

'Excellent. I'm so pleased to hear that. You must all be very relieved,' I said when Evie rang to tell me the good news about Zeke's progress. Rafe and I were inspecting the new huts.

'Yes, he's still not out of the woods, but the oncologist is really pleased. Zeke's white blood cell count is rising, and it looks like engraftment is happening. It'll be twenty-eight days before they know how successful it is, but everyone is upbeat, and he hasn't had any infections.'

'I'm so happy to hear that.' I gave Rafe a thumbs up.

'So, I'm coming home tomorrow,' Evie said, 'I'll be on the late afternoon flight. If there's any guests arriving on the same flight, I'll come over with Jiminy.'

'Okay, I'll check with Nell and let you know. If not, we'll come and collect you. How's it going with Jed?'

Evie paused and her tone changed. 'Fine. We're good mates. I haven't seen him much in the last week because he's gone back to work. And Zeke's in isolation, so I might as well come home.'

Disappointment filled me. I'd really hoped that Jed and Evie might have sorted out their relationship while she was down there. It was clear to anyone who saw them together they were meant for each other.

I was so excited about the progress of the building since Evie had left. The concrete had been poured for ten new huts, the restaurant, and the day spa, three days after Evie had left, and Rafe and I had met with the Riccardos.

The ten prefab huts had gone up last week, and the interiors would be finished by tomorrow, and ready for guests on the weekend. I'd interviewed and hired more cleaning staff, and Cherry and Mirabelle were starting as kitchen hands on Saturday along with a chef who was going to work as Tam's assistant.

'Look forward to seeing you tomorrow, sweets. And remember if you're still not one hundred percent, you're not working on anything!'

'Okay, see you. And I'm fine. All recovered. Bye.'

'All good?' Rafe asked.

'Yes. Her brother is good, but Evie sounded flat.

She and Jed haven't worked out, I don't think.'

Rafe put his arm around my shoulders as we walked towards the restaurant slab. 'You can't matchmake for everyone, love.'

'I know. I just hoped it would work out for her, but she'll be excited to see all this.'

'She will.'

'And guess what came today?'

'What?'

The signs for the huts, the day spa and the restaurant.

'The restaurant? I didn't think it had a name yet.'

'It does.' I nudged him. But it's a surprise for you.'

'Hmm. Do I like surprises?' Rafe pulled me close and dropped a kiss on my lips.

'You'll love this one!' I said, with my fingers crossed.

Chapter Thirty-One

Evie

After Evie finished her call with Pippa, she took a taxi to the hospital. Jed was still distant, and she didn't want to interrupt him, even though he'd given her his mobile number the first day she'd arrived.

In a way she was pleased; not seeing much of him was helping her adjust to the thought of leaving and going home to Pentecost Island. The last two nights she'd eaten alone, and she'd heard Jed drive in a couple of hours after she'd gone to bed.

The thought of leaving him was playing havoc with her emotions. The night before she'd gone to the hospital, she'd considered that maybe there could be a future for them.

But the next morning his face had frozen into an expressionless mask and she knew Jed had regretted his words of the night before.

Zeke was still in isolation, but she could stand outside his door and wave to him though the glass panel while she talked to him on the phone. A wave of love for her brother engulfed her as his face split into a wide smile and he picked up the phone.

'Hey, little sis. Good to *see* you!' Zeke's chuckle was loud. 'No aftereffects for you?'

'No, I'm back to normal. How are you feeling?'

'Really great, and looking forward to getting home. The doc's just been, and he reckons I can leave hospital and we can go to Jed's place in two weeks. Will you still be there?'

'That's why I came. I'm going back to the island tomorrow afternoon. Now that I know you're getting better I can keep in touch by phone.'

'I'll look forward to it. What about Jed?'

'What about him?'

'Ah, I guess that's a no, you haven't sorted anything out.' Zeke sounded disappointed.

'There's nothing to sort out,' she said briskly. 'Anyway, I just came to say goodbye, I'm going into the city to do some shopping. Tell Sam goodbye from me, and I'll talk to you when I get home. I love you, Zeke.' She put her hand to her lips and blew a kiss through the glass and smiled when he did the same from his bed.

##

Evie wandered around the Queen Street Mall looking for a wedding present for Pippa and Rafe. Jed hadn't mentioned making the outdoor setting for them again, and she didn't want to push it. To fill in time she went to the hairdresser, and in a sudden decision got her long hair cut off to a shoulder length bob, and then passed the time walking through dress boutiques until she found a dress to wear to Pippa's wedding.

But she had no success with a present and decided to look online when she went home. There was still three weeks until the wedding.

On the bus on the way back to the Bay, Evie stared through the window. The sun had disappeared, and a heavy grey sky hung over the city. Her mood matched it; she knew she'd been simply marking time in the Mall; she couldn't face the thought of going back to an empty house.

Jed was going to break her heart. Or maybe it was still broken from when she'd left him. It was no less than she deserved. Evie was more in touch with her emotions these days. Reconciling with Zeke, and seeing his happy family, and then seeing the new side of Jed had put everything into perspective.

She needed him in her life to be happy; she knew that now. But she had left it too late. Jed had made it quite clear that he didn't want her.

It was time to insist on a divorce so they could both move on.

The house was locked when Evie walked from the bus stop carrying her shopping. It was getting dark and there was still no sign of Jed. She let herself into the guest suite with the key he'd given her and put her parcels down on the bed.

She'd left a load of washing in the dryer before she'd gone to the hospital and she went to the downstairs laundry next to the guest suite to collect it. There was a basket of washing filled with Jed's clothes on the countertop, and she folded them after she had taken her clothes from the dryer.

Even though they had been washed and smelled of washing powder, she put one of Jed's T-shirts to her face and inhaled the sweet cotton aroma.

With a shaky breath, she put it down, and then collected his clothes with hers and took them back to her room.

Evie put her clothes in her suitcase, and then took the key that Jed had given her to the front door and took his washing upstairs. She walked through the house, appreciating the home that Jed had created.

Pushing open the door to the master bedroom, she walked in and put his clothes on the bed, and as she turned to leave, a photo on the bedside table caught her eye.

A happy smiling wedding photo. When Evie saw the look in Jed's eyes as he'd looked at her in the photo his friend, Boyd, had snapped, her heart broke all over again.

She walked out to the veranda and sat staring at the dark sky as unhappiness filled her. Eventually, she drew herself straight and pulled out her phone, and dialled Jed.

He picked up straight away. 'Evie? Is everything okay?'

'Yes, I just called to see what time you're coming back tonight.'

'Why's that?' His voice was cautious.

'I'm leaving tomorrow, and I want to talk to you before I leave.'

'Ah. I see. Just a moment.'

Evie frowned as she could hear him speaking to someone in the background, and a shaft of jealousy surged though her as she heard a female voice.

'Okay, I'm on my way now. I'll see you in a

little while.' The call disconnected and she stood there examining her feelings and thinking about what she was going to say.

***

Jed

It was only a matter of minutes before Jed turned his car into the driveway. Knowing Evie was leaving filled him with mixed emotions. He'd hardened his heart in a bid to protect himself; it was very clear that she didn't return his love. As he opened the car door, she stepped out of the door of the guest suite and he stared.

Shutting the door behind him, he said, 'What have you done?'

Evie reached up to touch the ends of the hair that didn't even reach her shoulders now. 'Oh, this? I had a haircut. It'll be cooler when I'm working at the resort in the summer.

'It's different. I don't mean to be insulting, but it's not you.'

Her eyes flared with anger. 'It is now.'

'Whatever suits you.' Jed shrugged and turned back to the car. 'I brought Chinese home. I was ordering when you rang.'

'Oh,' was all she said but a strange expression

flitted across her face.

'Are you happy to eat now?'

'Yes, and then I'll come down and get packed. I'm leaving early in the morning.' She followed him upstairs.

'I'll drive you to the airport.'

'There's no need,' she said. 'I can get a taxi.' Evie was standing beside him and it was hard to read her expression.

'I'll get the plates.'

All of a sudden, Jed realised, she was nervous. She'd said she wanted to talk to him, and he had a fair idea of what was coming.

He put the containers on the dining room table and headed into his bathroom to wash his hands. Staring at his reflection, he could see the tension around his mouth and the pain in his eyes. He'd thought it was hard letting Evangelina go in Bylington; this was going to be even harder this time, because he knew he loved Evie so much more now. She'd matured into a confident and beautiful woman; she'd shown strength in her reconciliation with Zeke, empathy with Sam and the boys, and courage in donating her bone marrow to save her brother's life.

But if it was what she wanted; he could do it. He would give Evie her freedom even if it broke his heart.

Again.

Running the cold water tap, he sluiced his face and prepared for the hardest conversation in his life.

Chapter Thirty-Two

Evie

They ate in silence, each lost in their own thoughts. Jed had offered to open a bottle of wine, but Evie had shaken her head. 'No, thank you.'

Wine was for celebration, and there was nothing to celebrate here tonight.

Jed pushed his plate away and looked across the table. 'I know what you want to talk about, and I'll make it easy for you. You want a divorce?'

She nodded mutely.

He held her gaze. 'Okay, we probably should have done it a long time ago, shouldn't we?'

'It wasn't for my lack of trying,' she said coldly.

His lips tightened. 'True, but it will be a lot easier now.'

'Easier? You really think so? How so?'

'The legal stuff, I mean. I'll see my solicitor this week, and I'll send you whatever is necessary. But there's one thing I won't let you say no to. I *will* pay you a financial settlement.'

'No. I don't want your money.' *I want you, Jed,*

her heart cried. Evie dug her nails into her palms and kept her voice even. 'I'll donate it to cancer research.'

'It'll be your money; you can do what you like with it.'

She nodded. 'I can.'

Grief sliced though her core as she looked at her husband for what might possibly be the last time. Was it likely she would ever see him again? Over the last three weeks her love for him had deepened, but she had to set him free. Could she really walk away from him and not look back?

Evie lowered her head. She took a deep breath and looked down at her hands twisted together in her lap. 'Let's not leave on bad terms, Jed. We were happy for a while, and I've really appreciated you looking after me while Zeke was in the hospital.'

'It was my pleasure. I'll miss you, Evie. It will be strange coming home to an empty house again.'

Evie's heart beat sluggishly, and her knees trembled as she forced herself to stand. If she stayed any longer, she knew she would break, and she couldn't let that happen.

Jed went to stand, and she waved him to stay seated. 'Stay there. I'm going to go to bed. My flight leaves early. I'll say goodbye now.' She held herself stiff and walked around the table. Putting her hand on Jed's broad shoulder and leaning down to brush a kiss across his cheek was the hardest thing she had ever done.

His hand come up and pressed against hers, but he didn't look at her.

'Goodbye, Jed.'

'Goodbye, Evangelina.'

##

Evie rose before dawn and called a taxi; she hadn't been to sleep at all and even though her flight wasn't until mid-afternoon, she didn't want to risk seeing Jed again. She knew she would break down if she did.

She asked the taxi to collect her at the intersection near the marina, and she left the key to the guest suite on the bedside table and closed the door quietly behind her.

As she walked to the footpath, she glanced up; the house was in darkness and she imagined that Jed was up there, deep in a relieved sleep. As she lifted her small bag over her shoulder and held her suitcase above the gravel driveway so the wheels didn't make a noise, the first tear rolled down her cheek.

##

Two hours later, Evie was sitting in a coffee shop in the terminal of Brisbane airport. Her bags were at her feet; it was far too early to check her luggage for the afternoon flight. Her coffee was cold and sat untouched on the table. She had lost her appetite, and her chest was dull and heavy. All she wanted to do was get back to the island and immerse herself in the gardens, and let herself heal. Getting over Jed was going to be difficult, but she knew she was strong enough to do it.

She would get herself together once she was on the plane. The wedding was only a couple of weeks away, and it would be a happy time on the island. Once the wedding was over, and the landscaping was all done, she would take *Kestrel* out and sail for a couple of weeks and lick her emotional wounds in private.

She jumped when her phone rang, and a glimmer of a smile stretched her lips slightly as she saw Zeke's name flash up on the screen.

Taking a deep breath, she injected brightness into her voice. 'Hey, Zeke. How are you today?'

'I'm fighting fit. They're really pleased with my progress. It looks like we've beaten this sucker together. You'll never know how much I love you for what you did, Evangelina.' The emotion in her brother's voice had her blinking tears away.

But they were happy tears.

'I'd do it all over again tomorrow, if I had to. I love you too, Zeke.'

'Okay, we've got the warm and fuzzies over, more to the point, how are *you*? Where are you?'

'I'm at the airport. Why?'

'I was just talking to Jed, and he said you'd left already. I thought your flight wasn't until this afternoon.'

'Um, yes, it is, but I wanted to get here early.'

'Pretty bloody early. Hang up, I'm going to Facetime you.'

'What? Why?' she asked but Zeke had ended the call. Her phone buzzed immediately, and she only accepted the audio call. She could see Zeke, but he couldn't see her.

'Turn your camera on and look at me, Evangelina,' her brother demanded.

'Why?'

'Because I want you to look at me when I ask you something.'

'What?' Her voice was thick, and she knew her

eyes were red from crying. She was getting it all out of her system before she got to the island.

'Do it.'

Evie sighed and touched the video button.

'You look like shit,' Zeke said. 'Why have you been crying?'

'Because.'

'You sound like you're ten-years-old. I remember that tone well.'

Evie smiled and stuck her tongue out at him, and he chuckled.

'That's better. Now tell me what's wrong. It's because you're leaving Jed again, isn't it?'

She nodded mutely. 'It was hard being back with him, but I'll get over it.'

'Just tell me one thing, sis. And then I'll leave you in peace. Do you love him?'

She bit her lip and nodded. 'Of course I do. I've never stopped, but I've left it too late. Jed doesn't want me anymore. Not fair, is it?'

'No, it's not. Okay, sis, you take care of yourself, and I'll talk to you when you get home. Sam and I have already talked about bringing the kids up for a holiday when I'm allowed to travel. I want to see this island that's worked its magic on you.'

'That's fab—' Before she could reply the screen went black. Zeke had disconnected the call.

Evie leaned her head back on the cushioned seat. She had chosen a table in a dark corner with a bench seat, and it was getting busy; she'd have to go and buy another coffee so she could keep the table. The terminal was noisy as the morning flights filled with passengers heading all around the country. She pushed her suitcase under the seat and walked over to the counter keeping one eye on the table.

A breakfast selection filled the glass display cabinet and she knew she'd have to force something down to give her the energy to get home. Maybe food would help dull the ache in her chest.

Evie took her eyes from the table and placed her order for another coffee and a ham and cheese toastie. When she turned and went to walk back to the table, she let out a quiet groan. A man had sat down at her table, his back to her. She hurried across and then stopped dead.

It was Jed sitting at the table waiting for her. Hitching her bag over her shoulder she turned away, looking for a sign to the ladies. She was going to be sick.

I can't do it again.

Hurrying blindly across the coffee shop, she came to a sudden stop as a hand gripped her arm.

Evie turned and looked into familiar blue eyes filled with concern.

Blue eyes that she knew and loved.

Blue eyes that were surrounded by laugher lines lit up by the wide smile on Jed's face.

Heat ran through her as she saw the expression in his eyes. No longer concern, but a tenderness that she had never forgotten.

'What?'

'Do you have something to tell me, Evie?' he repeated.

'Have you been talking to Zeke?' she asked quietly as he led her over to the table. She slid back into the seat against the wall and Jed followed her in. She was trapped between his bulk and the wall.

'I have,' he replied. 'And he told me that you didn't believe I loved you anymore.'

She nodded. 'I did. I mean, I do.'

'You were very wrong to think that, my love. Even if I have to sit here with you all day and all night to make you listen to me, so be it.' Jed reached out and took her hands in his.

'Why?' The first hint of sweet relief settled in Evie's chest as hope began to take root.

'I wasn't going to let you leave this morning. I lay awake all night and as soon as it was light, I came down and knocked on your door.' He laughed and shook his head.

'I stood there for a good half hour telling you everything I wanted to through that closed door, and then I saw the wheel marks from your suitcase in the gravel and knew that I'd been talking to a door. I'm not leaving until you believe me. I love you, Evangelina Stephenson.' Jed brought his face closer to hers and his breath whispered on her cheek. 'And then when I convince you of that fact, you're not leaving me.'

'I have to,' she said. 'I mean I don't have to leave you, but I have to go back to the island.

'Tell me one thing, and one thing only. Do you love me?'

'I've never stopped, Jed. Never, not for one minute. It broke my heart when I left you last time, and it broke all over again when I thought you'd stopped loving me.' She laughed through the tears that spilled onto her cheeks. 'I was even jealous of the lady in the

Chinese restaurant when I rang you last night.'

Jed was so close to her Evie felt the laugh rumble in his chest.

'I can't stay, as much as I'd love to. I have to go back and finish the landscaping for the wedding.'

He leaned back and pulled a white slip from his shirt pocket. 'I know you too well. I knew you'd say that. So, I'm not letting you leave me. I'm coming with you.'

Evie widened her eyes as happiness flooded through her. 'If there's nowhere to stay you—we—can stay on my boat.'

'It's all good. I've called Nell and I'm using up that five days credit I've got. But this time I booked a cabin for two. After that runs out, we might have to stay on your boat. I'll stay and help you with your landscaping. And at night, I'll lie with you, and tell you how much I love you. I'll never let you go again. Where you go, I go,' he said simply.

Evie threw her arms around her husband's neck and held him close. 'What about your work? You've been busy this week. Can you just walk away?'

'I'm my own boss, sweetheart, and I was busy filling an order for a woman who is very special to me. It was shipped to Pentecost Island this morning.' He grinned at her. 'Addressed to my wife.'

'You made the wedding gift? That's what you were doing?'

'I did.'

'I thought you didn't want to be with me.'

When Jed's lips claimed hers, there was no talking for a very long time. Eventually, Evie pulled back.

'Will you do one thing for me?'

'Anything, but first we have to ring Zeke and tell him we're married again.'

Evie shook her head. 'No, you have to do this first.' She reached down inside her T-shirt and pulled out the long chain that held her engagement and wedding rings. 'Will you put them on for me, please?'

'With pleasure, my love.'

Epilogue

Pippa

Saturday night in the Turtle Bar on Pentecost Island was shaping up to be a *big* night. The girls had decided to throw a pre-wedding party for Rafe and I—two weeks before our upcoming wedding—as well as a belated—by eight years—wedding celebration for Evie and Jed.

'You don't have to do this for us,' Evie said hanging onto Jed's arm. He'd barely left her side since they'd arrived three days ago. I'll never forget the feeling of joy that rose in me when I waited on the wharf with Tamsin on Tuesday afternoon for Evie to arrive on Jiminy's boat with three other guests, as well as Tam's new sous chef, Angus Alexander.

Seeing Evie nestled in Jed's arms as the boat came into the bay was a very happy moment for me—one of the many highlights of our time on the island.

If anyone deserved happiness, it was Evie, and I'll never forget the look on her face when she saw that the ten huts had gone up, and then the smile when she found out that she and Jed were booked into one of the new huts for a honeymoon.

She was a different person to the tense woman who'd left the island to go down to Brisbane to see if she was a bone marrow match for her brother.

The lights were on around the bar when Rafe and I strolled down after sunset. We'd both dressed up in honour of the occasion, and when we walked in, I was pleased to see we weren't the only ones who had made an effort.

Sienna and Eliza were wearing colourful dresses, and both had a hibiscus flower tucked in their hair.

I nudged Rafe. 'Look. You could have tried harder, boyo. Phillipe is wearing a tux.'

Rafe chuckled. 'He is, but at least I have shoes on.'

I giggled as I looked at Phillipe's tanned, but bare feet.

Nat and Gabe were deep in conversation across the bar. Nat grinned and held up a bottle of bubbles as I walked over.

'Of course,' I said with a grin. 'I hope you two aren't talking work.' I looked around. 'Where's the girls?'

They both laughed.

'Where do you think?' Gabe said. 'Nell's in the office and Tam's supervising the new chef. We both have workaholic partners.'

I rolled my eyes. 'They're both supposed to be off duty! That's why Angus came over early, and why I've got Mirabelle manning the office. I'll go and hurry them up.' I walked out past Sienna and Eliza who were talking to one of the couples staying on the island. Being Saturday night, we'd also have a few of the yachties come in for a drink and finger food. I smiled at the older couple.

'Welcome to Ma Carmichael's.' After a brief chat, I turned to Sienna and Eliza. 'Save us a big table before it gets too busy, please girls. Nat's cracking the bubbles. I'm just going over to hurry up Tam and Nell.'

It was a beautiful, clear night and the moon was high in a brilliant sky. The solar lights in Evie's gardens were directed up towards the huts, and they looked welcoming in the soft light.

Happiness trickled through me as I compared what I was seeing now to what the island had looked like on our arrival almost twelve months ago.

We've done well, I thought as I approached the

old house where the kitchen was currently housed. As I walked up the steps I frowned.

'I will not work under this . . . this . . . monster. If I'd known you were going to be here, Angus Alexander, I would have run a mile.' Cherry's voice was shrill and at full volume.

As I hurried into the kitchen, Tamsin's soft, calm voice was drowned out by the words of Angus, the new sous chef.

I walked in to see him wielding a huge knife and pointing it at Cherry.

'If I'd known that this incompetent, lazy, dishonest woman was on the island, I would have packed my bags and run as fast and far as I could,' his deep voice boomed.

'Look at him, this is assault,' Cherry screeched. 'He's threatening me with a knife.

'Oh, for God's sake, both of you,' Tam yelled. 'Would you please calm down.'

I stepped in, pulled a saucepan off the hook above the countertop and banged it on the bench. 'Immediately,' I said, loud and controlled.

Three heads, one exasperated and two with angry, red faces turned to look at me.

'Just what the hell is going on in my resort?' I said coldly.

THE END

All for one, and one for all.

Cherry Chilcott has always dreamed of being a chef. When she is offered a traineeship at the new resort restaurant on Pentecost Island, her dream is within reach. Tamsin Jones, her boss, is an award-winning chef and Cherry is keen to follow in her footsteps.

When Angus Alexander takes on the job as sous chef at the restaurant, he becomes Cherry's supervisor. Little does Tamsin know that this pair have a history, and it ended badly—very badly.
Can Cherry ignore the sparks that still ignite between them, and can Angus learn to trust the woman he once loved?

Come and spend some more time with the girls on Pentecost Island.

OTHER BOOKS from ANNIE

Whitsunday Dawn
Undara
Osprey Reef
East of Alice

Porter Sisters Series
Kakadu Sunset
Daintree
Diamond Sky
Hidden Valley
Larapinta
Kakadu Dawn

Pentecost Island Series
Pippa
Eliza
Nell
Tamsin
Evie
Cherry
Odessa
Sienna
Tess
Isla

The Augathella Girls Series
Outback Roads
Outback Sky
Outback Escape
Outback Wind
Outback Dawn

Outback Moonlight
Outback Dust
Outback Hope

Sunshine Coast Series
Waiting for Ana
The Trouble with Jack
Healing His Heart
Sunshine Coast Boxed Set

The Richards Brothers Series
The Trouble with Paradise
Marry in Haste
Outback Sunrise
Richards Brothers Boxed Set

Bondi Beach Love Series
Beach House
Beach Music
Beach Walk
Beach Dreams
The House on the Hill

Second Chance Bay Series
Her Outback Playboy
Her Outback Protector
Her Outback Haven
Her Outback Paradise
The McDougalls of Second Chance Bay Boxed Set

Love Across Time Series
Come Back to Me
Follow Me
Finding Home
The Threads that Bind
Love Across Time 1-4 Boxed Set

Bindarra Creek
Worth the Wait
Full Circle
Secrets of River Cottage

Four Seasons Short and Sweet
Ten Days in Paradise
Follow the Sun

Others
Deadly Secrets
Adventures in Time
Silver Valley Witch
The Emerald Necklace
Christmas with the Boss
Her Christmas Star
An Aussie Christmas Duo (two Christmas novellas)
A Clever Christmas

Acknowledgements

A special thank you to my wonderful editor and critique partner, Susanne Bellamy, and my eagle-eyed proof-readers, Roby Aiken, Nicki Edwards, Anna Welch and Kristen Woolgar.

About the Author

Author of the Year Ausrom Readers' Choice 2014

Best Established Author Ausrom Readers' Choice 2015

Finalist for Author of the Year, Book of the Year, Cover of the Year, Ausrom Readers' Choice 2016

Best Established Author, Ausrom Readers' Choice 2017

Book of the Year (Whitsunday Dawn) Ausrom Readers' Choice Awards 2018

Annie lives in Australia, on the beautiful north

coast of New South Wales. She sits in her writing chair and looks out over the tranquil Pacific Ocean. She has fulfilled her lifelong dream of becoming an author and is producing books at a prolific rate.

She writes contemporary romance and loves telling the stories that always have a happily Ever after. She lives with her very own hero of many years and they share their home with Toby, the naughtiest dog in the universe, and Barney, the rag doll kitten, who hides when the grandchildren come to visit.

Stay up to date with her latest releases at her website: **http://www.annieseaton.net**

If you would like to stay up to date with Annie's releases, subscribe to her newsletter on her website.